HIS TO CLAIM

BEARS OF GRIZZLY RIDGE

ELENA AITKEN

INK BLOT COMMUNICATIONS

ALSO BY ELENA AITKEN

Ever After: Volume One (Books 1-4)

The Springs Series

Summer of Change

Falling Into Forever

Second Glances

Winter's Burn

Midnight Springs

She's Making A List

Summit of Desire

Summit of Seduction

Summit of Passion

Fighting For Forever

The Springs Collection: Volume 1

The Springs Collection: Volume 2

The Springs Collection: Volume 3

The Springs Complete Collection - Books 1-10

Destination Paradise

Shelter by the Sea

Escape to the Sun

Hidden in the Sand

The McCormicks

Love in the Moment

Only for a Moment

One more Moment

In this Moment

From this Moment

Our Perfect Moment

Stand Alone Stories

All We Never Knew

Drawing Free

Sugar Crash

Composing Myself

Betty & Veronica

The Escape Collection

Vegas

Nothing Stays in Vegas

Return to Vegas

Timber Creek

When We Left

When We Were Us

When We Began

When We Fell

Castle Mountain Lodge

Unexpected Gifts

Hidden Gifts

Unexpected Endings - Short Story

Mistaken Gifts

Secret Gifts

Goodbye Gifts

Tempting Gifts

Holiday Gifts

Promised Gifts

Accidental Gifts

The Castle Mountain Lodge Collection: Books 1-3

The Castle Mountain Lodge Collection: Books 4-6

The Castle Mountain Lodge Collection: Books 7-9

The Castle Mountain Lodge Complete Collection

Halfway Series

Halfway to Nowhere

Halfway in Between

Halfway to Christmas

CHAPTER ONE

IT WAS one of those January mornings in the mountains where it looked as if everything had been dusted with glitter overnight. There wasn't a cloud in the sky and the sun blasted over the newly fallen snow, making it sparkle with a brilliance that hurt your eyes. Some people would call it magical. Kade Jackson was not one of those people.

He shrugged into his parka and pulled a knit cap over his head before he grabbed the thick leather gloves off the table by the door. He was headed out to clear the snow that had accumulated overnight.

Normally it would be his older brother Luke's job to drive the plow and make sure the driveway and parking area were clear of snow and ice, but Luke's mate, Chloe, was back from a business trip and Kade wasn't totally insensitive to the fact that they hadn't seen each other in a week. He also wasn't completely clueless about the fact that he likely wouldn't see either of them for the majority of the day. They'd be locked up in their cabin doing—he didn't want to think about it.

But he couldn't help but think of it. It had been too long since he'd scratched his own itch down in town. A very long time. A fact his bear reminded him of more and more these days. It didn't seem to matter how much he tried to squelch the animal inside him; it just got worse. A lot worse.

His bear wanted out. Needed out. His brothers would say it was making him crazy by keeping his animal at bay the way he had for so long, but there wasn't any other option. The shifter in him would cause nothing but trouble. Just the way it had for his twin sister, Kira. Because of her bear, she'd allowed herself to fall for a *fated mate*—not that he necessarily believed in that— and she'd run off to a different clan, tearing their family apart.

Because of Kira and her shifter blood, Kade and his brothers had been banished from their clan and were now trying to make a life on Grizzly Ridge.

It's a good life.

But it wasn't the life they were supposed to have. Alone. Away from family. And all because of one choice. But even as he trudged through the knee-deep snow and felt the bite of the cold air on his nose, he couldn't complain about the way things had turned out. At least, he couldn't complain too much. He did miss his family: his grandfather, cousins, and everyone else back in Jacksonville. Mostly he missed Kira. A lot. Sure, he had his brothers, and he was grateful for that every day, even when they made him crazy. But there was a bond between twins that couldn't be ignored. Especially in bears. From the moment she'd left, he'd been missing a piece of himself.

"No point thinking of that now," he muttered under his breath and tucked his face down into his parka a little farther. "Won't change a thing."

And it wouldn't. But it didn't stop him from thinking of it. *Every. Day.*

With it being so cold, and the blizzard from the night before so fresh, Kade didn't plan on seeing his oldest brother, Axel, or his mate, Harper, either. At least not for a while. Harper was struggling with a difficult pregnancy—little cubs could do that— and considering they didn't have any guests until the weekend, there was no real reason for anyone to brave the frosty morning.

Which was exactly why Kade *was* up. Shifting into his bear and enjoying a good run on the ridge would definitely be the best way to satisfy the discontent inside him, but since he'd taken that off the table as an option, it was best if he was alone as much as possible. He wasn't totally ignorant to the way his brothers and their mates looked at him lately. Concern all over their face—pity even. He knew they all thought all his problems could be cured by a shift.

They were wrong.

He made his way to the back door of the garage where they stored the truck and plow. There were footsteps in the snow, and a small path already cleared. No way Luke had left Chloe's bed on a morning like this one. He pushed his way into the garage and was immediately greeted with a blast of warm air. And Axel.

"Morning, brother."

Kade pulled off his knit cap and ran his hand through his hair. "What are you doing here?"

The truck had recently been parked, the engine still warm, snow dripping from the sideboards. Axel lounged against the workbench and poured himself a cup of coffee from a thermos. "I was just going to have a cup of coffee. Want one?"

Kade nodded and walked closer, but tilted his head in the unanswered question in the air.

"I just finished the drive," Axel said as way of explanation.

"The drive?" Kade accepted the coffee with a nod. "You plowed the drive?"

"I did." Axel raised his own mug in a toast but shrugged and took a sip of the brew when he didn't get one. "I knew Luke would want to stay in this morning."

"That's why I'm here."

"I wasn't sure you'd be so eager to do it this morning either."

Something in his brother's tone had Kade's instincts on alert. What was left of his instincts, anyway: over a year of not shifting into his bear had dulled his senses and his instincts considerably. It was starting to be a bit concerning. Not that he'd tell his brothers that. "Why wouldn't I want to plow the drive? I don't mind."

"I know. But today is a little different since..."

"What the hell are you not saying, Axel? We're a little too old for the games, don't you think?" Kade slammed the mug down on the counter. The hot liquid sloshed over his hand. He didn't flinch. "Tell me what's going on."

"The new cook arrives today," Axel said simply.

"Fuck."

He'd totally forgotten. And part of him had hoped that he'd finally made his point about hiring a chef when that was clearly his job. It had been a subject that Axel and Luke wouldn't let go in the busy fall season, but Kade had made himself more than clear at Christmas time that he not only didn't need help, he didn't want it and it wouldn't be welcomed.

"Well, I don't know if that's the best attitude, little brother. A little help in the kitchen might be just what you need."

"Need for what?"

"To relax." Axel put his coffee down and made a move to walk toward him. A move Kade quickly blocked with one hand up.

"I don't need to relax. I don't need to shift and I sure as hell don't need a mate, Axel. So back off. Now."

Almost anyone else would have been intimidated by Kade. He was a big man at six foot three and two hundred and sixty pounds of solid muscle. His time in the mountains and mostly self-imposed time alone had only added to his tough guy look, with a scruff of beard on his chin that he mostly didn't bother to shave off and a slightly wild look in his eyes. He knew exactly why his family was concerned about him, and his appearance was definitely on the top of the list. But as his big brother, and the alpha of their small little cast-off clan, Axel wasn't intimidated. He only shrugged. "I'll back off when you admit you need a little help."

"I do not need help." He gritted the words out through clenched teeth. "What I need is for all of you to leave me alone."

"What you need, *little* brother, is to own your bear. Someone in the kitchen to take the load off will give you the time to figure out what the hell is going on with you so you can sort your shit out once and for all."

"My shit is just fine." He turned and stalked to the far end of the garage. A little distance was what he needed if he was going to keep his fist away from his brother's face. Not that a little fight wouldn't feel really good right about now. *Really* damn good. But no. Kade stared at the garage wall for a moment, taking the time to collect his thoughts. "I thought we decided not to hire a cook."

"No," Axel said slowly. "*You* decided not to hire anyone. I made an executive decision. Well, along with Harper, Luke, and Chloe. We all think it's for the best. Not only for you, but also for the Ridge and our guests."

"The guests eat just fine." He still wouldn't turn around.

"Yeah, they do. It's the attitude of the cook that's not so great. We can't have you flying off the handle all the time, Kade. You're like a bomb that's just waiting to detonate. It has to stop. You can show the new chef the ropes and start slowly if you want, but like it or not, you're getting help. Today."

"The last thing I want is some other guy in my kitchen screwing with anything." He turned and glared at his brother.

"Good." Axel smirked. "Because I didn't say anything about the new chef being a *guy*."

Gabriella Santos navigated her little rental car up the slippery road, over-steering for at least the dozenth time when the wheels skidded on the ice. She'd convinced herself that despite the fact that she hadn't driven a car in the last few years, it wouldn't be a problem to get herself up to Grizzly Ridge on her own. After all, driving a car was a lot like riding a bike, right? One of those things you never forgot? And maybe it wouldn't have been so bad if it wasn't for the blizzard the night before, and the fact that not only had she never driven in snow and ice, she'd only ever actually experienced it one other time. And that barely counted considering she was only eight when her parents had taken her to the mountains in Chile. And that was very different than this.

When Gabriella had stumbled upon the ad for a chef at a mountain lodge in the middle of the wilds of Montana, she'd jumped at the opportunity. It had seemed like the perfect solution for her problem. A problem that involved getting as far away from her clan in Argentina as possible. She hadn't considered things like the weather, or the logistics of getting to the lodge. None of that seemed important. The only thing that was important was that the mountains of Montana were thousands of miles away from the hills of Argentina, her family, and more importantly, where Carlos Murez was. That was the only detail that mattered. Everything else—the snow, the ice, the complete and total remoteness of where she was headed—none of it mattered. As long as she was safe.

The fact that the place was called Grizzly Ridge— surrounded by bears, much larger bears than her own bespectacled bear clan—was a detail she'd also carefully considered. It definitely couldn't hurt. Especially if they were all as friendly as Axel Jackson, the alpha she'd spoken to on the phone. He knew vaguely of some of the clans in South America, but didn't know hers specifically. A fact she liked. A lot. It was best if he, and everyone else she met, believed her cover story of wanting to travel and see the world. Besides, it wasn't entirely a lie. She did want to see the world. But not as much as she needed to escape the bonds of a strong patriarchal society that cared more about mating her to the *right* bloodline than they did her personal safety. She'd been promised to Carlos since they were both cubs, a fact that Carlos had always taken to mean he could do with her what he liked. And usually what he wanted was to use her as a personal punching bag when he'd had too much to drink.

She'd had enough. Which was why she'd run. It was time to start over, and that was exactly what she was going to do—if she could make it up to the lodge without skidding off the road into the valley below. Gabriella hadn't let herself get excited about where she was going, not until she was on the plane to the States. Getting out of Argentina had been tricky, but she'd accomplished it with a series of bribes and moving quickly, mostly at night, until she got over the border to Chile and on the plane to Miami. Once she was stateside, it was easier to move around, but she'd still taken a twisted web of flights and bus rides across the country until she'd arrived in Billings, Montana. She'd seen more in the last two weeks than in her entire lifetime. Not that she'd had time to enjoy it. But she would. Gabriella fully intended to enjoy every part of her new home in Montana. She'd flipped through magazines and books during her travels that showcased the rugged beauty of the wilderness. It was so different from everything she knew. It was perfect. But first she had to get there.

She tightened her grip on the steering wheel and started to ease her way around the next bend in the road. But the tires had other plans and slipped on ice she couldn't see. No matter how much she turned the wheel to the right, the car continued to move in the opposite direction. In a panic, Gabriella slammed on the brakes, but that only seemed to accelerate the car through the turn.

She screamed as the little car whipped around again as if it were a carnival ride. The world, white and frosty, flashed past the windows in a blur. The last thing she remembered was thinking how she would never see the ridge and the views of the mountains that were supposed to be her new home. She closed her eyes and braced for impact.

His blood pumped hot and hard through his body so he could feel every beat of his heart and every single nerve ending throughout his body. It had been a long time since Kade had shifted into his bear, but he recognized the feeling. He needed to shift; his body felt as if it were literally on fire. The feeling came on hard and fast while he was talking to Axel. Something was wrong. His instincts, as dulled as they were, were raging.

Ignoring his brother, who was mid-sentence, Kade pushed his way out the door and into the frigid January air. He stuck his nose up in the air and sniffed, knowing it would be more effective if he used his bear. Axel was right behind him.

"Do you smell that?"

Axel shook his head. "What are you—"

"Try."

"What's going on?"

"Just try," Kade snapped, losing his patience. "Something's wrong."

He looked as though he might protest again, but Axel shook his head and did as Kade requested. "I...I'm not..."

"Shift."

"What?"

Kade could barely think, the blood was rushing through his head so quickly. All he could focus on was the sensations of his body wanting to rip apart around him and the instinctual idea that something was wrong. Very wrong.

"Axel, I need you to shift so your senses are stronger."

His brother crossed his arms over his chest and glared at him. "You shift."

Kade shook his head sharply. It wasn't an option. He didn't deserve to shift. Not since he'd failed at keeping his sister in the clan. He'd failed his family, and he wouldn't risk the chance that he would do it again. He no longer deserved to indulge in his bear. And Axel knew it.

"There's no time for this bullshit right now, Axel. Just do it."

With a sigh and another glare from his brother—which told Kade in no uncertain terms that he'd have to deal with Axel later—his big brother finally did as he requested. He disappeared back into the garage, no doubt to stash his clothes safely, and returned a moment later as a formidable dark grizzly. His nose was already working at the air, and then when the furry beast froze and snorted a sharp snarl, Kade knew he was correct. Something *was* wrong. Axel took off a moment later, down the road. Torn, Kade looked between his brother's lumbering bear form and the garage where the truck was.

"Dammit."

Giving in to his stubbornness, Kade went for the truck and followed as quickly as he safely could.

Gabriella fluttered her eyes open. Slowly at first, and then a bit more when she heard the snuffling. Scared that something might be broken, she moved slowly, turning her head first to one side and then to the next. That's when she saw it. A giant bear head looked through the passenger window of her car.

Where am I?

Confusion clouded her brain as she struggled to remember where she might be and what she was doing in a car.

Snow.

Snow?

Snow!

It came back to her in a flash. She was in Montana. The roads were icy. She went off the road. She looked back to the bear and the friendly eyes looking back at her.

It had to be one of the Jackson brothers from the lodge. The idea that she was calmed by a giant grizzly bear looking in her car struck her as funny and a giggle bubbled out of her throat.

The grizzly bear head shook side to side and then turned away.

"No!"

Gabriella's laughter turned to panic and she screamed for the bear to come back. "Help! Oh *Dios mio*! Please."

Hot tears slid from her eyes. When she moved to wipe them away, a sharp pain flashed through her left arm. *Broken.* She must have hit it on impact. *So the impact was hard enough to break a bone, but not hard enough for the air bags to go off.* The thought was so random, it almost made her laugh again. But the appearance of a new face, a human male face, at the window dried up the laughter in her throat.

He was the most handsome man she'd ever seen. His dark eyes looked right at her, calming her almost at once with a steady presence. His dark hair was shaggy and a bit wild, but it only seemed to match the scruffy beard on his face. It seemed strange to be noticing the appearance of her savior with such detail, but there was something about the man.

And then he spoke.

"Are you hurt?"

She was too stunned by the fire flowing through her body at the sound of his voice to answer him. Her body felt as if it might just explode right then. She hadn't shifted into her bear since puberty, a common practice for her clan, but she remembered distinctly what it felt like, and shame and fear immediately flooded through her. *Was she about to shift? Right there in the car? In the middle of a rescue?*

More tears slid down her cheek.

"Hey!" The voice came again. "Are you okay? Don't worry. I'm going to get you out of there."

His voice had a calming quality on her and she believed him. He'd get her out of there. Gabriella forced herself to take a deep breath and then another, until the tears stopped.

"Okay, I'm going to open the door," he said. "I just need to clear the snow away, okay?" She nodded. "I'm not going anywhere." He disappeared from view, but she could hear him working and talking to someone and then he was back and the door was opening. But not easily. He pulled and tugged and finally it was open. "I got you. Can you come across to me?"

She stared at him, momentarily unable to speak. His scent washed through her, flooding her senses. Despite the fact that she'd just been in a crash and was now in what could be a very precarious situation, she was totally frozen. And most definitely not from fear.

"Hey." His voice startled her out of her fog. "Are you okay?"

Gabriella nodded sharply. Whatever he was—or more precisely, whatever effect he'd just had on her—would have to wait. She clearly had more important things to deal with. Like her personal safety. She twisted to undo her seat belt, but with her broken arm, she couldn't manage it. "I can't...I can't quite..."

"I've got it." The next thing she knew, the huge man

crawled in through the passenger door. As he got closer, his scent grew stronger. Pine, like a Christmas tree, but earthier. It was unlike anything she'd ever smelled before, and her whole body strained toward him. "Don't struggle." The man reached across the console, and released her belt. "There," he said. "Now, let me take your—"

His hand rested on her good arm. Even through the down of the parka she'd bought in town, she could feel her skin light up from his touch. Gabriella swallowed. He was watching her intently, his face hard, unreadable.

She couldn't be sure how long they stared at each other. It may have been minutes, or mere seconds. And judging by the way they'd both locked in, it could have gone on indefinitely if it hadn't been for the car shifting under her. The movement spurred both of them into action. His hand clamped down on her good arm and he pulled her easily out of the driver seat and with him out the passenger door.

The blast of cold air hit her the moment they were outside. It was cold in the car, but protected from the wind, it wasn't nearly as bad as being exposed. She looked behind her at her little rental car. The hood was buried in a snowbank and one back wheel was suspended in the air, but all in all, the crash wasn't too bad. Gabriella wrapped her good arm around her body, cradling the broken one, and scanned the road around them. It could have been so much worse. On one side of the road there was the imposing mountain wall, and on the other side, with the exception of the ditch she'd landed in, were sharp drop-offs into the valley below. *If she'd only been a few feet over, she could have...she would have...*

The thought sent a fresh round of shivers through her.

A second later, the man's arms were around her, warming her. "Are you okay?"

She nodded against his hard chest. Because the moment he touched her, she felt perfectly fine.

"You're freezing."

"I'm fine."

He pulled away and held her at arm's length for a second before he patted down her arms. When he reached the broken arm, which had already started to heal up, she flinched. It may be healing, but it still hurt.

"You broke your arm."

She shrugged, because it wasn't a question.

"I need to get you warmed up."

Before she could respond, he bent and scooped her up easily into his arms. Gabriella wasn't a large woman, but her petite build was ripe with luscious curves and she'd never considered herself the pick up and carry type of girl. Of course, all the men in her clan were much smaller than the one who currently had her in his arms. She'd never seen such a large, manly man before. And she liked it. As did the bear inside her.

CHAPTER TWO

HE HAD to get her to the lodge. He needed to get her inside and warmed up and...away from him. But the idea of Kade being separated from the woman he'd pulled out of the car and settled next to him in the cab of his truck made him crazy. He couldn't be separated from her. Which made it even more important that he did so.

Axel had already taken off, back to the main lodge, no doubt to alert the others. They couldn't risk letting the woman see him in bear form. Except...she was a bear, too. Of that, Kade was sure. What kind of bear...he couldn't quite pin down. He'd never scented anything like her before. And she was tiny. Curvy in all the right places, of course, but much smaller than the females he was used to. He snuck another glance at her. She had her arms crossed over her chest and was huddled up in an effort to get warm despite the heat blasting from the vents. She was still favoring her left arm, but it didn't seem to be bothering her very much.

A quick healer.

A shifter for sure.

But there were still so many questions. Not that he was

going to ask any of them. It was best that he stayed quiet. He didn't trust himself to speak. Not to her. Not when there was such an emotional storm raging inside him.

"Thank you," she said and he noticed for the first time that she had a slight Spanish accent.

He nodded gruffly, but still didn't speak.

"I've never driven in the snow before," she continued. Her English was perfect, and she was obviously working hard to minimize her accent. "I didn't realize it would be so difficult. And the—"

"You had no business driving in the mountains in a silly little car like that," Kade snapped and instantly regretted it, but he couldn't seem to stop himself. "You need a truck to be out here. At the very least, an SUV."

"Is that right?"

Kade expected her to maybe shrink away from his anger, or even cry after all she'd been through; instead, her tone was hard. *Intriguing.* He risked a look in her direction and immediately wished he hadn't. His body responded at once to the fiery look in her eyes. She stared at him in a way no woman had ever done before, with challenge flashing in her eyes, and it made him want her with a ferocity that almost had *him* driving off the road.

"That's right. In fact, you have no business being out here at all."

"*Usted es un hombre arrogante.*" She huffed and turned away.

A retort was on the tip of his tongue, but given that he had no idea what she'd just said to him, he opted for silence the rest of the way up the road. As he suspected, Axel and Harper waited on the porch. Kade pulled up as close as he could, put the truck in park and slipped out the door without bothering to turn the engine off.

He needed to get away. Axel and Harper would take care of the mystery woman. They would be better equipped to handle her anyway. Especially considering his feelings alternated between annoyance and extreme attraction. It would be safer in his cabin. Alone. He needed to be alone. He needed very badly to be alone.

"Whoa."

Kade's shoulder slammed hard into a solid mass. He didn't look up; he didn't need to.

"Where ya going, little brother?"

"Cabin."

"No deal." Luke grabbed Kade's arm and spun him around. "Axel said we all need to be at the lodge. Something about a wreck and—wait a minute. Weren't you there?"

Kade shrugged.

"It's a yes or a no."

Kade jerked his arm away and shoved his hands into his parka. "I was there."

"So what happened? Is she okay? Axel said her car went off the road and...wait a minute." His brother grinned. The type of grin that made Kade want to slap it right off. The kind of grin that only meant one thing. *Trouble.* "It's the woman."

"I don't know what—"

"Axel said you got all weird, like you knew something was wrong. You made him shift."

A growl deep inside Kade's throat rumbled, threatening to get out. "He sure had a lot to say."

"I think there was a lot to say." Luke nodded smugly. "What's with the woman?"

"Nothing." Kade wouldn't meet his brother's gaze, but he was pretty sure the lack of eye contact wouldn't matter. "She's fine. I left her there for Harper to fuss over."

"And I'm sure she's doing just that. But we better go check it out."

"Can't."

He tried to walk away again, but Luke once more grabbed his arm and this time he wasn't letting go. "Alpha's order."

Kade growled again, and this time, judging from Luke's laughter, he was pretty sure his brother heard it.

"Oh yeah," Luke said. "This is going to be good."

Dios mio! He made her crazy. He clearly had issues, but Gabriella didn't think he would leave her like that, sitting in the truck alone without even one word. Hell, she didn't even know his name. What kind of man didn't introduce himself after saving a woman? Not that she had much experience with being rescued, and the argument could be made that she hadn't introduced herself either, but that didn't matter. The point was, he clearly didn't have any manners and worse than that, he certainly didn't know how to treat a lady.

Not that she cared. Why should she? It wasn't any of her business if he knew how to treat a lady or not. Besides the fact that it was just common sense and common curtesy. That was the only reason she cared.

Thankfully, she was distracted from the lie she couldn't seem to convince herself of by the appearance of a man who looked a lot like her rescuer, but darker, and much more groomed and put together. He opened the door; the cold air from outside immediately blasted her.

"Hi," the man said. "I'm sorry about my brother." He waved in the general direction that the other man had taken off in. "He's not entirely housebroken." He turned his concerned gaze back to Gabriella. "I'm Axel and this is my mate, Harper." He moved aside to reveal a beautiful blonde woman who, despite her winter coat, was clearly swollen with pregnancy.

Gabriella noticed the use of the word "mate" and the distinct scent of the men and nodded, confirming her suspicions. She was among bears and although she was pretty sure that would be the case, knowing it for certain put her at ease.

"Axel, we spoke on the phone." She extended her good arm and let Axel help her down from the truck. "I'm Ella Rodriguez. Your new cook." She used her childhood nickname and her mother's maiden name, the way she had on the phone when she accepted her job. It wasn't the best alias, but she hoped it would be enough. Especially considering she was so far from home.

"Ella!" It was the woman, Harper, who called her name and pushed forward to embrace her in a surprisingly strong hug. "Oh, I'm sorry," Harper added, when Ella winced at the flash of pain in her arm. "Of course, you might be hurt. How stupid of me. Are you okay?"

"I'm fine." She smiled to prove it was true. "My arm is healing quickly. It hardly hurts."

Harper took a step back and glanced over at her mate. "So, you're a..."

"Bear," Gabriella finished for her. She looked to Axel for explanation. Surely Harper must have been able to scent her, the way she had with them. But, come to think of it, she hadn't been able to scent Harper.

"Harper's half bear." Axel put his arm around his mate and gave her a kiss on the forehead. "And Ella here is a bear from..."

"Peru." The lie came easily. Too easily.

"I didn't realize there were bears in Peru." Harper tipped her head.

"Bespectacled bears. There's not many clans left. Not like the bears up North here." Gabriella turned slowly in a circle, taking in her surroundings for the first time. "And it's gorgeous here. And cold. It's also very cold here."

"Of course." Harper smacked Axel's arm lightly. "How silly of us," she said. "We should get you inside to warm up. Being from Peru, this weather must be a total shock. You poor thing. Let's get a fire going."

The next thing Gabriella knew, she was bundled up between them and shuffled up the steps of a giant log cabin. Inside, the warmth hit her immediately as well as an innate sense of comfort and hominess. A large rock fireplace and chimney dominated the room, with overstuffed couches clustered around it. There was a smattering of bookshelves and small tables close to some of the walls and windows. But it was the cozy chair that drew Gabriella, and not just because it was closest to the roaring fire; something about it promised sanctuary. Even if it was just from the cold.

"Welcome." Another woman greeted them, coming from the swinging door that obviously led to the kitchen. She held an overflowing tray full of hot chocolate and snacks. "I'm Chloe." She was slightly smaller, with jet-black hair tied in a neat braid down her back. Curvy and gorgeous with a similar glow that Harper had. Gabriella could tell right away she was a bear as well, but different from the others.

"It's nice to meet you." She accepted a mug of hot chocolate and sat. "Are you a sister...or..."

"Oh no." Chloe shook her head. "I'm Luke's mate. He's the middle brother. I travel a lot for work, but Grizzly Ridge has become home quickly. And I hope you think so, too."

"I'm so glad to be here," Gabriella said with full sincerity.

"Oh, you have no idea," Harper said from the couch where she'd settled herself. "I can't even begin to tell you how much we've been looking forward to having you here. We've been desperate to have some help in the kitchen."

They may not have any guests that she could see at the moment, but from what Axel had told her over the phone, they were a guest lodge that only opened the summer before. "Have you been without a cook since you opened?"

Axel answered. "Oh no, we've had—"

"Me."

The voice sent a strong and immediate reaction through her. Gabriella turned toward the door and the sound of the voice. There she saw a large, darker version of Axel and another man. *Her rescuer.*

"They've had me," he said. Even from across the room, his eyes held her with their intensity. "And you're here to take my job."

CHAPTER THREE

HOW COULD he *not have seen it?* Despite all his objections, his brothers *had* brought someone in to be a cook. And not just anyone, but a *female* and a female *bear* who happened to have a very dangerous effect on him.

Kade wanted to roar and storm out and he probably would have if Luke hadn't sensed his need to flee and had positioned himself directly in the middle of the doorframe.

"Simmer down, big guy." Luke grinned. "She's not going anywhere—you might as well get to know her. And something tells me that even if you won't admit it, that's exactly what you want to do."

That was it. Kade spun, ready to punch his older brother to shut him up for good, but Luke anticipated his move and side-stepped neatly into the room with a chuckle.

"There you are!" Chloe crossed the room, sidestepped his brother and went directly to Kade. She looped her arm through his and with a quick wink in Luke's direction, led Kade into the middle of the living room. "I don't think you've been properly introduced to Ella yet."

Ella.

That was her name. He'd rescued her, sat next to her, felt his bear damn near erupt in her presence. But he hadn't bothered to ask her name.

"It's nice to officially meet you." She extended her hand but Kade couldn't take it. If he touched her, he wasn't sure he'd be able to let her go. Her scent, stronger now that they were indoors, filled him. She was spicy, like a chili pepper, but there was something sweet underlying the heat. Exotic. Everything about the woman was exotic: Wavy, dark hair that fell over her shoulders. Warm skin that reminded him of those creamy coffee drinks Harper always drank. Curves that begged him to put his hands on them. But it was her eyes that caught him. They were golden, with dark flecks. *Mesmerizing.* And unlike anything he'd ever seen. *She* was unlike anything or anyone he'd ever seen. His entire body was electrified. He couldn't focus. He couldn't think.

"Kade." Axel delivered an elbow to his ribs, jostling him out of his trance. "Are you going to introduce yourself to Ella or just stare at her all day?"

He blinked; a hard blush crept up his neck. He rubbed his hand over the spot, trying to pull himself together. To her credit, Ella still had her hand extended and didn't look the slightest bit offended. In fact, unless he was reading more into the situation than there was, there was a flush to her skin as well.

"I'm Kade." His voice came out gruff and thick. Before he could talk himself out of it again, he took her hand and instantly knew he'd never want to let her go. She made a noise that sounded like something between a squeak and a groan. His cock thickened in his pants in response. "It's nice to meet you." He managed to get the words out in what he thought sounded like a normal voice.

Ella yanked her hand away and quickly sat in the chair, tucking her hands underneath her. Kade immediately felt the loss of her touch. His instincts roared at him, filling his head with a thunder that made it hard to think of anything but throwing her over his shoulder, marching her up the hill to his cabin and claiming her as his own.

The thought was so completely unexpected that he stumbled backward and would have fallen if he hadn't backed up against the couch, where he sat hard next to Harper, who looked more than a little amused at the situation. She put her hand on his shoulder. "It'll be okay," she whispered in his ear. "I promise."

He should be livid: with all of them for bringing in a cook, with her for being his replacement, and with himself for acting like an idiot in front of her. But Kade couldn't think. He couldn't focus. He could barely breathe. All he could do was sit and stare at her while she answered questions from the others and chatted easily with them, as if they'd all known one another for decades instead of hours.

The time passed quickly; people came and went, brought in food, changed places on the couch, and discussed the details about the Ridge. But Kade barely heard the conversations going on around him. All he could focus on was the woman sitting a few feet away from him and how she went against everything he'd ever believed.

His family—his clan—had been pulled apart not once but twice because of mating and the idea that fated mates were worth risking everything else. First his mother chose a mate that her father, the clan leader, didn't approve of. They'd run off to raise their cubs alone, but when Kade and his twin sister were barely babies, their mother returned them to the Jackson clan and their grandfather. They hadn't seen or heard from her since.

The only one who knew where she was, and why she'd left them, was their grandfather, the alpha.

But he wasn't talking. Not to Kade and his brothers anyway. As far as their grandfather was concerned, they were dead to him too. All because Kira, Kade's twin, had chosen a mate he didn't approve of and the brothers had decided not to force her to return the way their grandfather had requested.

Mating did nothing but destroy families. He'd always believed it. He'd held firmly to that belief, especially since Kira left. Even when Axel found Harper and then Luke found Chloe, Kade still vowed he wouldn't let it happen to him. He would never put himself in any situation that would make him vulnerable to hurt. Not again.

But that was before.

Before he'd looked through the window of that crashed car in the snowbank and set eyes on...*her*.

All at once, everything was different. He was on unstable ground and he had no idea how to keep from falling.

He'd done little more than stare at her all day, and Gabriella was more than aware of him. She could feel his eyes watch her every move. His gaze warmed her.

No.

It heated her to the core. Her body was on fire for him and he hadn't even touched her. Well, not if you didn't count the handshake and sure, that simple contact had caused a storm inside her, but that was definitely not the kind of touch she was craving. Not from him.

She wanted his strong, confident hands on her body. She wanted his touch on her bare skin, exploring every inch of her in a way she'd never craved from anyone else before.

Gabriella did her best not to react or respond to Kade's attentions; at least, she thought she was doing a good job, but she didn't miss the little smiles and knowing glances between the others. Especially the women. But it didn't bother her. The only thing that bothered her was the turmoil roiling through her body. Her bear clambered to get out. She couldn't remember the last time she'd given in to her animal. Not since she was a teenager and was busy rebelling against her father, running alone in the hills.

Females in her clan were taught to suppress their animal and to do what they were told. What their men told them to do. It was a culture Gabriella had never fit in to. Particularly once she got to know the man whom her father had arranged a union with. At first she'd just thought Carlos was a sleazy, weasel of a man. But as time went on, not only was her first impression of Carlos accurate, he also proved to be an abusive bully, too.

She was too strong for him. Too strong-willed. And he'd made it his mission to *get her in line* and *teach her what her place was*. When she told him what Carlos was doing to her, her father was no help. Not only did he not care that she was being abused, he blamed her.

"Be a good girl, Gabriella," he'd tell her. "You're to be his mate. If he feels he needs to teach you his ways, that's his right as your mate."

It wasn't.

It would never be any man's right to lay another hand on her.

Never again.

So she'd run.

Because nothing could be done simply, not when it could be extravagant, her father had arranged an elaborate mating ceremony for everyone to watch while she became Carlos Murez's mate. A match, he told her, that would benefit both of their clans, a solid bloodline match that would ensure the survival of their species. Something to be celebrated.

Whatever. She'd planned it perfectly and when the timing was right, the day before the ceremony when everyone was too busy with the last-minute arrangements, she'd run.

Now she was free and she was more than ready to explore that freedom. Not only that, her bear seemed to know it, too. And so much of that was a foreign feeling to her.

"Excuse me," Gabriella cut Harper off as she was explaining something about some upcoming guests they had scheduled in. She probably should have been listening, but she just couldn't sit any longer. Not for one more second. She jumped up from the chair. "I just need to..." She trailed off when she realized everyone stared at her. "*Lo siento,*" she added quickly. "Sorry. I just...could you maybe..."

"Why don't you come with me to see the kitchen?" Chloe appeared at her side and took her arm. "I can't believe you've been here as long as you have and we haven't even shown you where you'll be working."

Gabriella could have hugged the woman for giving her an out. "Thank you," she settled on. "That's exactly what I'd like to do."

Especially if it took her away from Kade so she could try to formulate a thought. She let the women lead her through a swinging door into the nicest kitchen she'd ever seen. It was both ready for commercial cooking but at the same time, warm and welcoming for guests. The glistening, commercial-grade stainless-steel appliances were a large presence in the prep area, with big slabs of polished concrete countertops. Gabriella's eyes were instantly drawn to the cooking area.

It would be a dream to prepare food there. Her chimichurri and empanadas, as well as all the American dishes her *abuela* back home had taught her how to make. As a girl, she'd spent a lot of time in the kitchen with her grandmother instead of with the other young girls. It was easier to immerse herself in the smells and tastes of good food than it was to pretend she fit in with the rest of the girls in the clan. As Miguel's daughter, she would never be like the others. She'd been different from the day she was born. Promised into a marriage, and considered more of a bargaining chip than a child, she'd never been completely accepted. Being in the kitchen was definitely easier.

"This is beautiful." She ran her hands along the counter-tops, and walked through the stools that sat at the counters, ready for guests to come down and drink their coffee and eat the fresh muffins she planned to prepare for them. And scones with her famous *dulche de leche* topping. Gabriella planned to bring a taste of her world into this world, but only a taste. She'd moved away from Argentina for a reason. Well, for a lot of reasons. As much as her culture was a part of her, she wasn't tied to it. She was ready for a change. In every way.

Kade.

A man hadn't been part of the plan. Definitely not been part of the plan. But she couldn't ignore the way he made her feel. And even if she could, she didn't want to.

"Kade designed it," Harper said.

Gabriella startled. She'd been so lost in her own thoughts, she'd forgotten the other women were there, and more importantly, that they'd also been in the other room and had witnessed the interactions between her and Kade.

"He did a great job," she mumbled and didn't meet their eyes.

"He does a great job on a lot of things," Chloe chimed in. "And he's a whiz in the kitchen. I think you two will work really well together. You'll be a perfect complement to each other."

"In more ways than one."

She couldn't help it. Gabriella turned to look at Harper, who smiled mischievously. "What does that mean?"

"Don't pretend you don't know," Harper said. "We all see it."

"Even Kade sees it." Chloe nodded. "And he doesn't seem to be rejecting it."

"Rejecting it?" The idea that Kade would reject her hadn't occurred to Gabriella. To be fair, she hadn't really thought beyond her own feelings for him. Feelings that she was more than willing to act on. And that alone both scared and thrilled her. "Why would he reject it?" she asked. "I don't want to be too forward, but...he seems to feel something, too. No?"

The women laughed.

"Oh, I think it's safe to say Kade feels something."

"We've never seen him like this," Chloe added. "I mean, not that I've known him as long as Harper, but..."

"This is different," Harper added. "Very different. We should have tea."

Gabriella wanted to scream. *No.* She didn't want tea. She wanted to know more about Kade and why it was different *now*. Why *she* was different. But she swallowed her impatience and let Harper show her where the tea was and where the mugs were kept. She was patient while it brewed and even while the cups were poured. And then she'd had enough. She couldn't wait any longer.

"Why is it different?"

Chloe answered. "Kade doesn't believe in mates or mating."

"And he definitely doesn't believe in fated mates."

"Nope." Chloe took a sip of her tea. "Definitely not."

Fated mates. That's what they were. Without a doubt in her mind, Kade was her fated mate. She believed. She very much believed. Even if she hadn't even one day ago. She did now.

"But now?" She directed the question to both of the women,

but neither of them answered. Instead, they looked at each other, exchanging a glance. "Well? Do you think he believes now?" Even as she asked the question, she already knew the answer. She knew just by looking at him.

He believed.

CHAPTER FOUR

"WELL, ISN'T THIS INTERESTING?"

"Very."

Kade ignored his brothers. He kept his stare fixed firmly on the kitchen door, where Ella had disappeared. She'd been in his life less than twenty-four hours and already his body rejected the idea of her absence. It didn't make any sense. But at the same time, it made perfect sense.

Mate.

She was his mate.

No.

Mates were nothing but trouble. They were more than trouble. They would ruin your life.

"I know what you're thinking." Axel's hand slapped on his shoulder, jarring him from his thoughts.

"No you don't," he growled.

"I do too." Axel moved so he stood in his line of vision. "You're thinking she's your mate."

"No."

"Yes you are." Luke joined Axel and they stood shoulder to shoulder. "We can see it all over you. She's your fated—"

"No!" Kade jumped up and paced the room. *This couldn't be happening.* Everything had been working out just fine before Ella had shown up. He was doing fine without a mate. He didn't want or need a female in his life. He ran his hands through his hair and tugged the roots. His skin was hot, itchy. He felt as if he were going to combust from the inside out.

"You need to shift."

"No."

"Kade."

"No!" He spun on his older brothers and growled.

Luke and Axel shared a glance but it was Luke who spoke. "I know you feel like you can't."

"I can't."

"You need to," Luke continued, as if he hadn't spoken at all. "It's the only way you're going to clear your head enough to think this through. Everything is just going to be worse if you don't."

"We think you're feeling everything more intensely with Ella because you've repressed your bear for so long," Axel said. "Which is remarkable in itself." He shook his head and again they exchanged a look. "The fact that you sensed her in trouble before you'd ever even laid eyes on her...that's something."

"It's nothing." The words tasted bitter as he spoke them. Of course it meant something. It meant *everything*. He'd never been so worried, so consumed with fear for another person as he was when he sensed Ella's distress. That definitely meant something.

"I don't know why you're fighting this, Kade, but I've had almost enough." Axel crossed his arms and glared at him.

His big brother rarely took a tone of authority with him. As much as Kade wanted to ignore it, he couldn't. But he didn't have to accept whatever he was saying.

"Enough of what, Axel?"

"Enough of all this." He waved his arm, gesturing over Kade. "You've been completely impossible to live with since—"

"Don't say her name," Kade warned.

"She's our sister, too," Luke said.

Kade shook his head. They'd never understand. "She's my *twin* sister." Twins shared a special bond in the shifter world. More so than any other sibling or any other connection. When Kade said good-bye to Kira and left her with her mate and his clan, he'd not only made the choice to go against his grandfather's wishes, he'd made the choice to say good-bye to his other half forever. It was a decision that haunted him every day.

But there'd been no other choice. Had they decided to force her to leave with them, it would have caused a war between the clans. A problem their grandfather didn't seem concerned about. But he also hadn't considered the fact that Kira was in love. She was mated. To her *fated mate*, she'd said. She couldn't fight it. She also couldn't explain it. Kade had begged her to explain her choice to him. Why she'd chosen to go against everything for a *mate*.

She couldn't.

She'd only looked at him, her eyes so much like his own, clouded with pain and all she said was, "I'm sorry, Kade. One day you'll understand. One day it will all make sense."

And he'd sworn then and there that he'd never let something that couldn't even be explained destroy a family. It wasn't worth it. It would never be worth it.

Ella.

Was she worth it?

His body and soul screamed one answer. His mind, another.

"Did you pick her because of me?" Kade turned and asked Axel.

"Who?"

"Ella," he said simply. "Did you pick her to try to mate me to her?"

Axel shook his head. His eyes were clear and didn't look away. "No," he said, and Kade knew he wasn't lying. "I picked her because she was the only one who answered the ad who had experience cooking for large groups and didn't sound crazy. Believe it or not, cooking at a remote mountain lodge isn't high on a lot of people's list of things to do."

Kade nodded, satisfied with his brother's answer.

"But I will tell you this," Axel added. "I didn't know for sure, but I got the sense when I spoke with her that she was a shifter. I'd be lying if I didn't say I wasn't hopeful that you'd get along with her. But I'll tell you what...I never could have dreamed it would go so well. I never would have guessed you'd be fated."

"We're not."

"Whatever. Just do me a favor, okay?"

Begrudgingly, Kade nodded.

"Don't fight it. At least not too hard."

"I'm so sorry it's not the most luxurious accommodation," Harper apologized for at least the tenth time. "But we have quite a few bookings from now until the spring, so we can't give you one of the guest rooms to stay in. As soon as the snow melts, the guys will get to work building you your own cabin."

"If they need to."

Harper glanced sharply at Chloe, who just giggled. Gabriella knew exactly why they thought it was so funny. She had to admit, she thought it was pretty funny that they were going to so much trouble to set her up in the little storage room where they'd shoved a single bed and a dresser. It's not that she objected to the surroundings at all. She was fine to sleep wherever. But the reality was, she didn't plan to spend any time there.

Heck, if she was right about Kade, she wouldn't even be spending one night in the little storage room.

"Something tells me they won't need to bother," Gabriella said and the other women's mouths dropped open. "Oh, don't pretend to be shocked," she said. "You both just finished telling me that you think Kade and I are fated, and I think so, too. So don't be so surprised that I'm ready to embrace it."

And she was. Where she came from, there was no need to dance around the subject. If two people felt they were fated, they acted on it. There was no *waiting period* or *courting* or whatever other North American ideas of waiting for an *acceptable* time frame had passed. They just moved forward. And that's exactly what Gabriella intended to do.

The others may not see it, or even believe that Kade was capable of taking a mate, but she saw it. Kade was capable. More than capable. And she would prove it.

"We did say that," Harper said. "But Kade isn't like the others. He's..."

"Sensitive."

"Sensitive?" Gabriella directed her question to Chloe. "Well, sensitive or not, I plan on discovering everything I need to about him. And then some. He's my mate. I know it. And he does, too."

"He does?"

"He does."

"Well, I wish you luck with him," Harper said. "I really do. I love Kade, and I think I can speak for all of us when I say that we just want to see him happy. He's denied his true self for so long, it's really starting to take a toll on him."

Her comment caught Gabriella off guard. She put her bag

down on the bed and sat next to it. "What do you mean? He's denied his true self?"

"He won't shift," Chloe said. "It's killing him, I think. If not killing him, it's making him crazy. Grizzlies need an outlet. He needs to shift, to run his bear, to...mate. The longer he goes without it, the harder it is on him."

"You're not a grizzly?"

Chloe shook her head. "I'm a black bear. I still need to shift, but it's not a consuming need like it is for the grizzlies. What about you? What's it like for you? I'm sorry to say I really don't know anything about bespectacled bears or your clans or anything. I don't really keep up with that side of the life."

"Don't worry." Gabriella laughed to cover her nervousness. It was definitely a good thing if they didn't know anything about her clan. "I obviously don't know anything about any other species. I've had kind of a sheltered life, to be totally honest." If she could stay as close to the truth as possible, she'd be fine. With the exception of the few very huge lies she'd told these nice people.

But the one thing she wasn't lying about was her feelings toward Kade. That was real. That was *very* real.

"To be honest, I haven't shifted in years. It's kind of discouraged in my clan. At least for females."

"No way!" That was Harper. She'd been reclining against the door, looking as if she might fall asleep, but that piece of news woke her up and caught her attention. "How could you not shift? It's the best thing. I can't believe I'd gone my whole life without it."

"So you can—"

Harper nodded excitedly. "I can. I didn't think I could, but I can and I love it. I thought the first time was the best, but I was wrong. It just gets better and better. To be able to run like that... totally free without any restrictions on you or—"

"Expectations," Chloe chimed in. "It is pretty remarkable. And we have the most beautiful country here. The ridge is like nothing you've ever seen, Ella. You have to check it out."

"Oh...I will. I mean, I want to. And I guess as soon as the snow—"

"Oh, no," Chloe interrupted her. "You have to go in the snow."

"I'm not really prepared for the snow." She gestured to her jacket that she'd hung on the hook on the wall. "I thought it would be warm enough, but it's really not. I guess I'll have to go down to town when I get a chance and buy some—"

"That's not what we mean." Harper smiled. "You need to go with your bear. You have to experience it that way."

Shift? There was no way she could do that. Or could she? Why not?

"I guess...I mean..." Both women looked at her expectantly, so she just spat it out. "Okay," she said. "Why not." She wiggled her arm. "And my arm feels better, so...can we go now?"

Chloe and Harper exchanged a glance. "I don't see why not," Chloe said.

"I'm so jealous."

"You're not coming, Harper?"

She shook her head and her hands went to her belly. "We don't think it's a very good idea while I'm pregnant. I'm only half shifter, and it takes a lot out of me when I do shift. Never mind how tired I am already. Carrying a cub is exhausting."

"I can imagine," Gabriella said, although she couldn't. On some level, she always thought she'd have cubs one day, but after she'd met Carlos and really discovered what kind of man he was, she'd taken steps to ensure she wouldn't get pregnant. And she wouldn't. Not as long as she took the herbs the medicine woman two villages over had given her. A warm glow moved through her as she realized that would no longer be a problem.

She was free.

Free from Carlos, his abuse, and a future that was anything but what she wanted. She hadn't had much time to process everything. She'd been too busy running and traveling and then there was the crash. But now that she was actually in Montana and at the ridge surrounded by such nice people, Gabriella could finally breathe.

She'd done it. She'd really done it. And it was better than she ever could have imagined. Especially considering not only had she found her freedom, she'd found her mate.

Gabriella felt bad that Harper couldn't join them, but she was so nervous about actually shifting, she couldn't dwell on it. Instead, she tried to remember how it had felt the last time she'd shifted into her bear. It was a long time ago, and she had trouble remembering the mechanics of it, but she could still very vividly remember the sensations that came once she'd shifted. Just...the feeling of freedom. As if nothing could hold her back or contain her. It was so hard to explain or put into words, but as she followed Chloe outside, every fiber of her body twitched and got prepared for the euphoria that was about to flood her.

"It's freezing out here." Gabriella wrapped her arms around her body and tried to control the shiver. From what she'd seen so far, Montana was beautiful, but it was also ridiculously cold. Never before had she experienced the kind of bone-deep cold she'd felt since she'd been in the mountains.

"I know. It's part of the problem with shifting in the wintertime." Chloe led the way through a packed trail toward a small cabin. "But it'll be worth it. I promise." She glanced backward at Gabriella and her face scrunched into a frown. "Are you okay? You look like you're going to shiver right out of your skin."

"I'll be fine." She managed to squeeze the words out between the clatter of her teeth. "Are we almost there?"

Chloe had told her they'd go to her cabin where they could leave their clothes on the porch and shift right into the trees, to avoid being spotted. It hadn't looked far from the back door of the kitchen, but Gabriella was quickly learning that even three minutes outside in the cold was three too many.

"It's right here. Come on." Chloe led the way up onto a porch and immediately took off layers. "Are you ready?"

"Absolutely." Without hesitation, Gabriella did the same and right after Chloe leapt off the porch, shifting into a sleek black bear, Gabriella closed her eyes and called on her bear. It had been so long, she wasn't sure her animal would respond right away, but she did.

Soon, the vibrations started; her core temperature rose and then...

Gabriella jumped off the porch in the direction Chloe had disappeared and felt her body transform. The second her paws hit the ground, she took off running. Her muscles stretched and reached for each step. Just as she anticipated, a fierce sense of freedom rushed through her, flooding her senses and filling her with a happiness she hadn't felt in years. Maybe ever.

She pushed her body, following the prints Chloe left; her paws sunk in the snow with every step. The icy slush covered her paws, leaving little stings and prickles on her pads. It was cold, but not painfully so. Not like before. With her fur, the snow slid off and cooled the heat of her body, making the winter air tolerable.

Chloe's tracks veered to the left. Gabriella followed and when the trees cleared, what she saw next took her breath away. She sat down hard and stared at the view in front of her. It was like nothing she'd seen before. Breathtaking wasn't even close to an appropriate word to describe it.

The trees opened up and exposed the view of the valley below. Towering snow-covered mountains surrounded them on all sides, and the ridge ran up to what looked like the top of the world. When she sat, it felt as if she could see the entire world from that one little spot.

It took Gabriella a few minutes to realize she wasn't alone. She swung her head around to see Chloe sitting next to her. She'd never seen a black bear in real life before. The only bears she'd ever seen were from her own clan, and even then, only the males. Chloe was beautiful. Her fur was so dark and shiny, it sparkled almost blue in the winter sun. She was a lot larger than Gabriella, but not nearly as big as she could imagine a grizzly was.

As Kade would be in his bear form.

The thought sent a shiver through her that seconds later turned into heat. She wanted him. Badly. She'd been so suppressed her entire life, she'd never felt the way she was feeling about a man before. But maybe that had less to do with her life and more to do with the fact that she just hadn't met Kade yet.

Either way, now that she had laid eyes on him, she was definitely not in a hurry to let him go. Quite the opposite, in fact. Gabriella had never thought of herself as a particularly forward person, but she also wasn't a shrinking violet. If there was something she wanted, she'd go after it. And now, in Montana, she was damned well going to make this new life everything she'd always dreamed about.

She surveyed her surroundings, her companion, herself. Hell, if she could shift and embrace her bear again, she could also embrace every other thing being a bear had to offer.

Including a fated mate.

She shivered again at the thought. It felt right. Very right. Maybe the girls thought Kade didn't believe in the idea of fated mates, but she could see the truth. And even if he did need a little bit of convincing, she was definitely the woman for the job.

Chloe nudged her, and made a grumble deep in her throat.

Time to go.

With another look out at the ridge, Gabriella reluctantly turned and followed her new friend back into the woods and in the direction of the lodge. The return trip didn't take long, which turned out to be a good thing since Gabriella could feel herself getting tired. And, admittedly, a little cold. Certainly the fur helped ward off the cold, but she had to remember she was a South American bear. She wasn't built for such cold temperatures. That would definitely be an adjustment.

She watched as Chloe jumped easily onto the porch, shifted seamlessly and disappeared into the cabin. Just like that, in the open. Of course, they'd said there were no guests on the ridge at the moment; otherwise, they would be a lot more secretive about the shifting. But as it was, it was only family. The Jackson family. And that meant, Axel and Harper, and Chloe's mate, Luke. And of course...Kade.

As if the mere thought of him had conjured him, she felt his eyes watching her; she sniffed the air and her head filled with his scent. She turned her head up the path, toward the last cabin. He was watching her. He knew she'd have to shift and he was waiting.

Another chill ran through her. She'd have to shift soon.

Fine.

Heat flooded through her, settling in her core. She'd give him exactly what he was waiting for. Taking a different approach than Chloe had, Gabriella moved to the bottom of the steps, where she knew Kade would have the best view. She shifted quickly, seamlessly, and stood for a moment, her back to him. She extended her arms over her head, allowing her naked body to stretch first one way and then the next. She could feel the intensity of his gaze watching her but she purposely didn't turn around as she moved slowly up the stairs, taking extra care to swing her hips and stick out her round bottom. She had to focus to ignore the pain the snow and ice was causing on the bottom of her feet, but the seduction was way too perfect. A few more seconds in the cold would be fine. It would be worth it.

The cabin door opened as she reached the top. Chloe appeared with a large wool blanket. "What are you doing? You're going to freeze to death!" Her eyes moved quickly over Gabriella's shoulder and she grinned. "Oh, I see." She shook her head. "Still. You're going to freeze. Here." She threw the blanket over her naked body and held the door open for her.

But before she followed Chloe inside, Gabriella turned and met Kade's eyes. Even from the distance, she knew she'd made her point.

He was hers.

CHAPTER FIVE

DAMN.

All the blood in Kade's body was currently concentrated in one spot and it was definitely not his brain. His bear roared just under the surface, desperate for a release. But there was only one release that would do.

One woman.

One mate.

Ella.

If she wasn't frozen to death by now. Silly woman. What was she thinking, shifting in the frigid air and then just standing there, with her naked body on display?

Oh, he knew exactly what she was thinking. And he definitely appreciated it. But it was way too cold for that type of behavior, especially for a bear from South America. Earlier, Ella had been shivering uncontrollably, and that was sitting in a warm truck with a layer of clothes and a warm parka on. She must be completely frozen now.

Without stopping to think it through, Kade double-timed it up the path to his cabin and skillfully lit a fire in the hearth before he grabbed a wool blanket off his couch and headed back out the door to Chloe and Luke's cabin, where Ella was.

He didn't bother knocking, but flung open the wooden door, truthfully a little harder than he meant to. When the door slammed against the wall, the women started.

"Kade? What the—"

"What were you thinking?" He ignored Chloe and marched through the room to where Ella sat. Just as he knew she would be, she was shivering. Her skin was pale, her eyes squeezed shut against the cold she was feeling. He could see the bare skin peeking out from under the blanket she was wrapped in. Her clothes were in a pile on the floor.

"I thought she should warm up a bit before she got dressed again," Chloe said in explanation to his unasked question. "I didn't realize she would react that way to the cold. I didn't think—"

"No," Kade growled. "You didn't think." He wrapped the extra blanket he'd brought with him around her and scooped her easily into his arms. "She's not from here, Chloe. She's not built for snow and cold."

"She wanted to," Chloe said, stopping him before he walked out the door. "I should have prepared her better for the cold, but she wanted to shift, Kade. I don't think she's the type of woman who'll do anything she doesn't want to do."

That was true. He may have just met Ella, but he felt as if he'd known her forever. She'd been in his soul, in his heart, his entire life. Her weight shifted in his arms and cuddled closer to him. Kade tightened his grip on her. "I think that's true," he said to Chloe and then looked down at Ella. His mate. "No, I know it's true. But now it's time for something I want to do."

Ella shivered, but Kade knew it wasn't from the cold this time. Without another word, he walked out the door and as quickly as he could on the slippery snow and ice, made his way up to his cabin, where he slammed the door behind him. One hand held her securely against him; he used the other to toss a pile of pillows on the floor in front of the fire and placed Ella in the center of them.

He didn't have a full kitchen because he spent the majority of his time in the lodge kitchen, but he did have a corner stocked with the basics, including a liquor cabinet. He poured out a dram of whiskey, fetched two more blankets from the closet in his bedroom and stripped his clothes off before he joined Ella in front of the fire.

If she noticed his nakedness, she didn't say anything. She was so cold, he wouldn't be surprised if she wasn't really sure where she was or what she was doing there. He'd fix that in a hurry. Kade shuffled in behind her, spread his legs and pulled her back so she rested against his chest. It was a very intimate position, especially considering they'd only just met, but it didn't feel out of line. Not in the slightest. And when Ella wiggled herself backward into him, he knew she felt it, too. Everything about having this woman in his arms felt absolutely right.

Except for the fact that her body was freezing cold.

"Drink this." He handed her the glass and she took it obediently. "It'll help take the chill out of your bones."

She took a sip and to his surprise didn't immediately sputter and cough. Kade twisted around so he could see her face. "A whiskey drinker?"

Ella shrugged a little and took another sip.

Kade shook his head and smiled to himself. Especially now that she was talking again. She must be warming up. But not fast enough. "What were you thinking, standing out there like that?"

Her answer was a smile so sweet and sexy his entire body ached. He slipped his hands up her back and slowly massaged her shoulders, easing some warmth back into the skin before he slid his hands down the length of her, to her waist and then the swell of her ass.

"You could have frozen to death," he said. "You're not used to this cold."

"But I didn't."

She wiggled a little, so he kept his hands moving. Up and over her shoulders and down her bare arms. With every touch of his own overheated skin, the ice in hers melted a little more.

"No." Slowly, Kade brought his fingers up the length of her arms, and instead of traveling back to her shoulders, he trailed them along her chest. Over the mounds of her breasts. "You didn't." His cock twitched in response to the feel of her under his fingertips. It was bold. Bolder than he might normally be. Especially with a woman who mattered. Not that he'd ever been with a woman who mattered. But his boldness didn't feel inappropriate. It was right. She was right. "I'd never let that happen." And he meant it. It didn't matter that she'd only just entered his life; he knew with a fierce certainty that he'd never let anything happen to this woman. She was his to protect, to care for, to...*claim*. The idea was still so foreign he couldn't wrap his head around it.

There'd be time to come to that later. First...he had a naked woman in his arms and he planned to take full advantage of that.

He squeezed first one breast, and then the other, taking time to roll each nipple between his fingers, massaging gently with just enough pressure to make sure she warmed up. Ella groaned and leaned her head back against his chest, presenting her luscious lips for him to take with his own.

He wanted this woman. No, he *needed* this woman. But to kiss her? That was different. Wasn't it? He didn't normally kiss the women he took to bed. It was a line of intimacy he never crossed. But...with Ella...

It was different. It was *all* different.

She'd been so cold she couldn't even think properly. The last thing Gabriella remembered was showcasing herself for Kade outside on the porch. She'd wiggled and flaunted herself without any care for the biting cold. That had been a mistake. *Or had it?*

Sure, she may have almost frozen to death. But she hadn't. And now she was sitting between the very firm, very muscular legs of the sexiest man she'd ever laid eyes on. With every touch of his hands on her bare skin, not only did Gabriella warm up a little bit, she damn near exploded from the heat he stirred in her. She hadn't been with a lot of men before Carlos, but Kade's touch was unlike anything she could have even imagined. He was both gentle and commanding, and just so...right. She let herself fall into the feelings he was awakening within her. A low groan started deep within her, and slipped out between her lips as she leaned her head back against his chest.

Her lips throbbed for him. She wanted his mouth on hers. To taste him. To connect.

He looked at her and Gabriella could see the internal battle going on inside him. *Over a kiss? Or was it more? Was it her?* The others had warned her that Kade had demons that even they didn't fully understand.

Demons or not, this man was her mate. She felt it with every bone in her body, even more so since she'd let her bear out. She'd never been the type to shy away from what she wanted, especially now that she had this new life in this new land. She'd have everything she wanted, she'd never been so sure. And what she wanted was Kade. If he had demons to battle, she had every intention of going to war with him.

She twisted in his arms until she was face to face and looking in his eyes at the surprise there. He wrapped his arms around her and she pressed her breasts into his chest. Kade opened his mouth, but she didn't have the patience for anything he had to say to her. She pressed her lips to his in a hot, hard kiss that left no room for thought of any kind.

His hands were on her back, her ass...everywhere. Kade's touch was hot, frantic, and totally in control all at the same time. There was no doubt he needed her just as much as she needed him.

Maybe more.

"This is crazy." He worked his way down her neck with searing kisses.

"There's nothing crazy about this."

"We just met." He nestled his face between her breasts. The scruff of his beard sent shocks of pleasure through her body. "I don't usually..." He trailed off and she knew it was a lie. Of course he'd had one-night stands before. She didn't care. What was happening between them was definitely not a one-night stand. Far from it.

"I don't care what you did." She arched her back to present her chest to him. "All I care about..." Kade cupped her breasts and sucked first one nipple into his mouth, teasing her into a hard peak, and then the other. "Is exactly what you're doing..." Liquid heat pooled between her legs. She wiggled her hips, pressing herself against his hard heat. "Right..." Kade's hands locked around her hips to lift her and when he brought her back down and onto his hard shaft, she threw her head back, the word coming out on a moan. "Now."

He filled her so completely she wasn't sure she could move. Her eyes squeezed shut as sensations ripped through her.

"Look at me," he commanded.

She wasn't sure she could. She shook her head slightly.

"Now."

A shiver rippled through her at his commanding tone. She liked it. A lot. Slowly, she lifted her head up, opened her eyes and stared directly into his.

"Better," he said when she finally looked at him. He needed to see her, connect with her. Ella was different than any woman he'd ever met. Everything about her—about them, their connection, their intensity—everything was different.

Slowly, he moved beneath her. Ella's eyes fluttered.

"Keep them open," Kade told her. "Look at me. Don't look away."

He slid his hands over her; his thumbs stroked circles on her soft belly while he rocked inside her. "Damn, woman. You feel so..."

He let his words trail away instead of finishing his thought. He couldn't. There was no way Kade trusted himself to say what he wanted to. What he was feeling. If he did, he'd say something he shouldn't. It was too soon to say what he wanted to. What his heart and mind strained to tell her.

Too soon. That was an understatement. It had been less than twenty-four hours and already there was no doubt in his mind that this woman was his. His mate.

No.

He bit back the urge to tell her that.

He didn't believe in fated mates.

And he'd just keep telling himself that until he believed it again. Because at that moment, with Ella straddling him, the feel of him inside her so intense he had to focus to keep from losing himself, it was hard to remember why exactly he didn't believe in mates.

Very hard.

Ella's eyelids fluttered; a deep moan escaped her lips. His bear reacted hard to the sound of her pleasure. He pulled her closer, and buried his face into the crook of her neck where he could fill his senses with her sweet scent. He nibbled and kissed his way down her neck and paused at the tender skin just below her ear. He could take her. Right now, like this. He'd mark her, claim her for his own. She was his, and in just an instant she'd be his forever. He swallowed back a roar and jerked his head away.

No.

He couldn't do it.

He wouldn't do it.

Having her this way, that was one thing. Sex was something he could control. Mating was different. Confusion clouded in her eyes and something else. *Hurt.*

She'd wanted him to. But it didn't make sense. He couldn't mate her. But he didn't want to see that pain in her eyes either.

His brain battled with the feelings crashing through him. There was only one thing to do. Kade reached up and pulled her mouth down on his. He kissed her hard until she responded with as much need and want as he had flooding through him.

With one arm wrapped around her, he lifted her and shifted around until she was beneath him. Exactly where he needed her.

"Kade...I...you...we..."

With a wicked grin on his lips, Kade rose up on his arms, slowly pulling himself from her wet heat. Ella's eyes widened, and she was about to protest when he pushed back inside her. Hard.

"*Dios mio.*" The words were little more than a groan. He

gave her a moment to adjust to him again. She bit her bottom lip and opened her mouth to say something, but he was done talking. Once more, he withdrew from her, and with even more force than before, they came together. She moaned, hard, and Kade could see the battle in her eyes. She had something she wanted to say, but the pleasure was slowly erasing it from her consciousness. He did it again. And then again. Until he could see in her eyes that Ella's only focus was on him and the pleasure he was giving her.

And the feeling was more than mutual. He felt her body tighten and shake beneath him as a scream of pleasure ripped through her. Moments later, his own orgasm tore through him.

Sometime later, as the fire burned low and he held her in his arms, asleep against his chest, Kade stroked her dark hair off her forehead and placed a gentle kiss there before gathering her closer to him. It didn't matter how many times he told himself it was just sex. It wasn't and he knew it in his bones. He may not have claimed her, but there was no doubt about it: Ella was his mate and that meant more than just the act of mating. That meant that everything he'd ever believed in was wrong. And everything had just changed forever.

CHAPTER SIX

WITHOUT A DOUBT, being with Kade was the best thing for Gabriella about being at Grizzly Ridge. But in the days and weeks since she'd arrived, she very quickly found there were a lot of other benefits to her new life. A lot. Chloe and Harper proved very quickly to be some of the best friends she'd ever had. No, they definitely were the best friends she'd ever had. Growing up, it wasn't easy for her to make close friends because of who her father was, and she'd never known the closeness of a female relationship before. She could hardly believe she'd missed out on it for so long.

The other women took her under their wing and showed her all the ins and outs of the Ridge and life in the mountains. Which was another huge benefit of being in Montana. The mountains were amazing. She couldn't get enough of them and didn't think she could ever get tired of looking at them. And running along the ridge in her bear. Embracing her animal once again was definitely something she had fully embraced. Almost every day, she took time to shift and go for a run. Usually with Chloe, but when she traveled for work, she'd go with Luke or Axel, or even once or twice by herself. She couldn't convince

Kade to shift and go with her. His brothers told her he was punishing himself for something that happened with his sister, but he wouldn't talk to her about it.

In so many ways, he was open to her. They would talk and laugh for hours into the night. And during the day, Kade was more than patient as he explained things in the kitchen, and they compared recipes and blended their cooking styles to create delicious feasts for the guests. More than once, Axel and Luke had each taken her aside and told her how much Kade had changed since she'd come to stay at the ridge. No one thought he would be as open to working with her as he was. Of course, no one expected her to be Kade's mate either. Least of all Kade.

Not that they'd officially mated. She wanted to. More than anything, she wanted him to claim her, but she wouldn't ask him. No. He'd have to come to it on his own, and clearly something was stopping him. Chloe and Harper told her that he didn't believe in mates, but he did. That's why they were together. That was the only reason they could be together. But he wouldn't take the next step.

So many times, Gabriella had wanted to ask him about it but she'd chickened out at the last minute. After all, who was she to challenge him when she wasn't being totally honest with him either? Every day, she'd wake up in Kade's cabin, where she'd stayed ever since that first night, never spending not even one night in the little storage room bedroom they'd set up for her when she'd arrived, and she'd look at the man she had fallen in love with and convince herself that today would be the day she'd tell him the truth about who she was and where she'd come from.

And every day, she'd change her mind. There never seemed to be a good time. Something was always happening at the ridge. They were fully booked with guests and that meant her days were full of cooking up warm soups and freshly baked breads for them to enjoy when they came in from whatever snow-shoeing or skiing trip Luke had taken them on. The evenings were consumed by visiting as a group before they'd cuddle up in front of the fireplace in Kade's cabin. It was perfect.

But today was the day. She'd been at the ridge for a month already. And it was time to come clean. Besides, Gabriella had the crazy idea that maybe if she told Kade everything about who she was, that maybe he'd be able to overcome whatever block was keeping him from claiming her and they could finally be mated. But first, she had to get through the day. And it would be a busy one, which was why she'd slipped out of bed and made her way down to the lodge before Kade had woken up.

Luke was taking the guests on an all-day snowshoe trek, which meant they'd need packed lunches as well as a warm dinner when they returned. And there had been a special request for Gabriella to make a cake for one of the young guests to use in a wedding proposal after dinner. It was going to be busy, but also extra romantic and she had the perfect idea for a cake to make. Which meant she needed to get busy if she was going to have time to decorate it perfectly.

With perfect timing, only moments after she put the cake in the oven, the door opened and Harper, dressed in leggings and a t-shirt that hugged her growing belly, came in and joined her.

"You're up early." Gabriella poured her friend a cup of peppermint tea and slid the mug in front of her.

"Coffee," Harper moaned. "Why can't I just have a coffee?"

"You know why." Gabriella plated a fresh cinnamon bun and handed it to Harper. "It's not good for the *bambino*. Here. Maybe this will help. I made them this morning."

"Sugar is better for the baby than coffee?" Harper raised an eyebrow in her direction but tore off a corner of the fresh bun.

"Fresh baking is *always* better." Gabriella laughed. "Especially if it's *mi abuela's* famous recipe."

"Your grandma?"

Gabriella nodded but turned away. She'd been really careful about how much she'd said about her family, but more and more, little details started to sneak out. The more comfortable she felt with the Jackson family, the more she told them. And that could only lead to trouble if she wasn't careful.

"Were you close to your grandma back in Peru? Was it sad to leave? You don't say much about your life in South America."

Gabriella busied herself by cleaning the cake bowl and putting the dishes away so she wouldn't have to look at the other woman. But Harper didn't seem to notice Gabriella's avoidance as she munched on her cinnamon bun.

"Of course it was sad," Gabriella answered honestly. "But sometimes a change is exactly what you need to live your best life. You know?"

"I completely agree with that. For me, it was getting rid of a gay husband and finding a bear." The other woman laughed so genuinely, Gabriella turned around and joined in. "But I suppose it wasn't that dramatic for you?" Harper asked.

"No. It wasn't quite like that."

"Well, no matter what brought you to Montana, we're sure glad to have you. And not just for these yummy buns either. I don't know what kind of spell you've cast on Kade, but he's like a completely different man since you've shown up."

Gabriella poured herself a cup of tea and leaned on the counter. "That's what everyone keeps telling me."

"Because it's true. And like I said, I don't know how you convinced him that mating wasn't the terrible evil he seems to think it is. Or, I should say...the evil he *thought* it was."

"Oh, we haven't mated." Gabriella bit her lip. She didn't want Harper to know how much it bothered her that he kept stopping short of making her his.

"You haven't? I'm sorry." Harper's eyes filled with something Gabriella really hoped wasn't pity. She couldn't handle that. Besides, there was absolutely no reason for anyone to pity her. She had Kade. Whether he wanted to mate with her or not, she had him and she had this amazing new life at the ridge and she was happy. She didn't need him to make it official.

Except she did. And it was more than just her pride and her heart. If she was mated to Kade, even if Carlos found her one day, he wouldn't be able to do anything about it. He'd have to leave her alone. Not only would she be happy—she'd be safe.

It wasn't the first time Kade had woken up to find Ella already gone. Sure, he preferred to wake her up with a snuggle, a caress or two and a nibble on the back of her neck that would lead to a steamy wake-up way better than any cup of coffee could be. But he also knew that some days she liked to get an early start on the kitchen and that usually meant fresh cinnamon buns. He definitely wanted to be sure he got one of those buns before the guests got them all. But first he should take a side trip to the shed and see whether his brothers needed any help with the plowing.

Having Ella around was supposed to free him up from spending all his time in the kitchen, but it really had just accomplished the opposite. Because of Ella, the kitchen was the only place he wanted to be. As long as she was there.

The sharp bite of the winter air hit him, but Kade didn't feel the cold. He left his parka unzipped as he trudged through the snow. His body was always running hot these days. In fact, since Ella had shown up. He'd never been more satisfied, in every way, but there were other differences as well. His body temperature, for one. It was almost as if he were burning up from the inside. All the time. His thoughts were often muddled and confused. He'd go through moments of clarity, followed by instances where he was putting sugar instead of flour into the gravy. He'd never been the type to be forgetful or not on top of his game, especially in the kitchen. To say it was unsettling would be a gross understatement. But that wasn't the most concerning of the changes he'd experienced since Ella had come into his life.

No, it was the way he was completely willing to give up everything he'd been holding on to as truth since Kira went away. It may not have made any sense to his brothers, but Kade's complete disregard for his bear and everything that went with it had been exactly what he'd needed to keep from going crazy with the grief of losing Kira. Holding on to the anger and almost hatred for his animal and everything it represented, including the idea of mating, was just the fuel he needed to stay sane. But what he felt for Ella was anything but sane, and it was getting harder and harder to keep his bear away.

She'd only been in his life for little over a month, but already he couldn't imagine if she wasn't at the Ridge. But at the same time, he couldn't imagine how she could possibly stay. Not if it was going to make him crazy to be around her. He was damned either way.

"Good morning, little brother."

"What brings you here?"

Both of his brothers turned to greet him when Kade opened the door of the shop.

Immediately, the heat from the building assaulted him and he stripped off his jacket. "Thought you might need a hand. Maybe I'll shovel out the side yard."

"The side yard?" Axel glanced at Luke and they exchanged a look. "I can't imagine any reason we'd need the side yard in February, Kade."

"We talked about putting a volleyball net up there for the guests. It could be fun."

"In February?"

"Why not?" He growled and grabbed a shovel. Maybe with a bit of physical exertion, he could settle whatever was brewing inside him. He needed to do something.

Axel shook his head. "Time for a coffee?"

"Just water. Cold."

Luke threw him a bottle from the fridge. "What's up with you?"

He didn't answer, just chugged the water down. It wasn't enough. He gestured with his head and Luke tossed him another one. "Thirsty," he said when he was done.

Axel mumbled something under his breath and Luke chuckled.

"Something to say to me?" He growled at his older brothers. They should know that if he was fixing for a fight, he'd get one. His muscles twitched at the idea of connecting his fist with something. Even if it was one of his brother's faces. He'd always been the one out of the three of them to jump to physical aggression to solve his problems. Something about being the youngest, needing to prove himself, his grandfather used to say. But since denying his bear, the aggression had only gotten worse because it was the next best thing to shifting to relieve some of the pressure. He didn't even care whether he got pounded by them; he had to do something or he would explode.

"Settle down." Luke smirked. "I thought having a mate would finally bring you into line. I don't know how she manages to live with you, but shit, man, you're just getting worse."

He hadn't told them he wasn't mated with Ella. He didn't think he'd have to. Really, they should have figured it out on their own. Kade looked away and growled.

"Wait." Axel put his hand on his shoulder, but he shrugged it off. "You're...you didn't....how have you..."

"Fuck."

"What the hell is wrong with you, Kade?"

"Wrong with me?" He swung around, ready to throw a punch but when he saw the way his brothers looked at him, his anger faded, replaced by an overwhelming wave of defeat. His shoulders slumped and he shook his head. "That's just it," he said. "I don't have any fucking idea. She's not my mate." He told them the truth before he changed his mind. "I mean, she is. She *is*. But we...I...we..."

"You haven't claimed her yet," Axel finished for him.

"No."

"Because you think somehow that makes you weak?" Luke asked, disgust laced in his voice. "Do you think that allowing yourself to open up to a woman and take her into your heart is some kind of weakness? That's the very thing that makes you strong. What exactly is your problem?" He rose up in front of Kade, clearly ready to give him the fight he was itching for.

Kade flexed his hands into fists. "I never said it made me weak." He looked right into Luke's eyes, knowing exactly what would piss him off. "You did."

His older brother growled and took a step closer. "I know what you want, little brother. And if you think that poking a stick at this bear is going to get you the fight you think you need, you're wrong. But I'll tell you one thing."

"I'm sure you will."

Luke ignored him and kept talking. "You think you're better than us by ignoring your bear? You're not."

"That's not—"

"Whatever the fuck you think you're doing by denying who you really are, all you're doing is making us all fucking crazy. Including yourself. And if you're not careful, you're going to lose the best goddamn thing that's ever happened to you because you think your bear is some kind of liability. It's part of you. An important part and the sooner you realize that, the better off you'll be." Luke swung out and punched the door next to Kade's head. "Hell, the better off we'll all be." Luke grabbed his parka and stormed out. The door slammed behind him.

What the hell did he have to be so pissed off about? It was Kade who couldn't stand to be in his own skin, Kade who was itching for a fight to calm his bear, Kade who had everything he didn't even know he wanted, standing right in front of him. But it was going to slip away because he couldn't for the life of him get past the idea that if he embraced it, it would ruin everything.

CHAPTER SEVEN

AFTER SHE'D TALKED to Harper, Gabriella felt more confident in her decision to tell Kade the truth. It was time—long past time—and she knew in her heart that he wouldn't care what she had to say to him; he'd still feel the same way about her. Maybe he might even be ready to take the next step and claim her. Her body shivered with the idea of being his forever.

Definitely, it was time to tell him the truth about who she was, and then Chloe and Harper and the brothers, too. The Jacksons were quickly becoming her family. She'd be safe with them. Carlos couldn't find her. And even if he did...

Despite the fact that Gabriella had made her decision to come clean, she still had a job to do. And apparently she had to do it by herself. Kade hadn't joined her in the kitchen the way he usually did. Axel came in for a coffee and said something about him shoveling out the side yard, which didn't seem to make much sense, but there was a lot about American men that didn't make a lot of sense to her.

"Hey, Ella?" Instead of returning to his office right away, Axel lingered in the door, his coffee in his hands.

"*Si?*"

"Can I ask you a question?"

"*Si.* Of course." She grabbed a towel and wiped her hands before she grabbed the cooler for the lunches she'd prepared for the guests' expedition.

Axel hesitated for a moment, and for a brief second she thought he might know the truth about who she was. Fear flashed through her. She swallowed hard and forced a smile. "What would you like to know?"

"It's not really a question, I guess," he said. "But I should tell you..."

She nodded, waiting for him to continue.

"Kade isn't shoveling the side yard," Axel said. "He's gone."

"Gone?" The word was dry in her mouth. Like sand. She reached for a glass of water. It shook in her hand but somehow she managed to get some water into her mouth before she set the glass down. It jostled and spilled on the counter, but Gabriella didn't care about the mess. "Where did he go? When will he be back?" The more important question was, *will he be back?* But she couldn't bring herself to ask. Fear numbed her. She couldn't feel her feet yet somehow she was still standing there.

"Everything's fine." Axel took a step toward her, but it was cautious. "He just needed to go away for a bit."

"A bit?" The fact that she hadn't felt his absence until the moment Axel said something worried her. She should have known. She should have felt it. But they weren't mated. They hadn't strengthened their connection. And now... "Where did he go? Why do I feel like you're not telling me something? Why wouldn't he have said good-bye? Told me himself?" Too many questions but Gabriella didn't care whether she sounded like a crazy person. She *was* a crazy person. At least she would be if she didn't get some answers. "Axel? Tell me what's going on."

Somehow she registered his hand on her shoulder leading her to a chair. "Ella, please don't worry. It's nothing to worry about. I'm sorry—it's my fault. I didn't really approach this in the right way."

She shook her head.

"There was an argument this morning."

"Argument?"

Axel nodded. "A brother thing."

"Of course."

"I gave him an ultimatum," Axel continued. "I told him if he didn't figure it out, he couldn't stay on the Ridge."

No. Gabriella felt as if she'd been punched in the gut. *He had to stay.* He couldn't leave but if he did, she'd go with him. "Wait. What does he have to figure out?" She was pretty sure she knew the answer, but she needed to hear it.

"Kade's always been...well...intense." She nodded and Axel continued. "And after he met you, we were kind of hoping he'd settle down some—and he has. But he's also gotten a lot worse, too. In a different way."

She knew exactly what he was talking about. *Kade's demons.*

"Where did he go?"

"To see our grandfather."

"*Tu abuelo?*" She didn't know much about the Jackson patriarch, just that he'd banished the brothers from the clan because their sister had mated against his wishes. He sounded a lot like her own father. It scared the hell out of her. "*Por que?* Why?"

"He needs to figure things out on his own. Maybe this will be what he needs. Maybe he'll get the answers he's looking for. Or..."

"Maybe he won't," she finished for him.

Gabriella didn't have time to dwell on Kade's absence. A fact she was grateful for. Even if Kade was gone, she still had a job to do and she'd do it to the very best of her ability. If he'd wanted her to go with him, he would have asked. But he didn't. She wasn't going to pretend it didn't sting, because it did. But if he needed to get away, that was his business. At least that's what she was going to tell herself. Ultimately, she needed to trust him and that he was going to do the right thing for both of them. And she did.

The day passed quickly, if not a little quietly. It was different working without Kade at her side. As if the women knew she would be struggling, which they likely did, they took turns coming in to talk to her and keep her company while she decorated the cake that would be used for the proposal later that night.

"So he's going to propose with a cake?" Chloe was perched on the stool and watched as Gabriella smoothed a layer of buttercream over the surface. "Doesn't that seem kind of cheesy? I mean, what's he going to do? Hand her the cake and watch her eat it until she bites into the ring? Where is the ring? Can I see it?"

Gabriella tried not to laugh at her new friend's opinion. It did seem a bit cheesy, but every couple was different and she certainly wasn't going to be the judge of what romance was. Not when she didn't have a ring on her finger, or even a mate of her own. The thought stung a little, so she pushed it away and focused on the conversation.

"I don't have the ring," she said. "And to be honest, I don't really know what his plan is—just that he needed a cake to pull it off."

"Well, that's definitely a yummy-looking cake," Chloe agreed. "And it'll be an interesting evening, that's for sure. I'm glad I get to be here to see it. I leave again in the morning."

"Again?" Gabriella felt a twinge of disappointment. She didn't want anyone else to leave, but at least with Chloe, it was for work. "I don't know how you can travel so much and actually like it."

"It keeps my bear happy to be on the move." She shrugged. "And it's okay to leave when I know I always have a home to come back to. I never had that before. It makes me want to come back. And who knows...maybe someday I'll have a little something to slow me down a bit and stay put."

Gabriella almost dropped her spatula. "What? Really?"

Chloe laughed. "Settle down. I'm not pregnant. Not yet anyway. But watching Harper go through it, I might be changing my mind a little."

"Really?"

"Don't you think it looks...I don't know...*nice?*"

It was Gabriella's turn to laugh. "I don't know if I'd use the word *nice* to describe it. And I'm pretty sure Harper wouldn't either. But..." She knew exactly what Chloe was talking about. Seeing Harper, with her swollen stomach, knowing there was a cub growing inside her, sparked an instinctual need for her as well. One she never thought she'd have. But things were different with Kade. "Yes," she said. "I do think it looks nice."

She couldn't help but wonder whether Kade would think the same thing.

"You've thought about it too?" Chloe asked. "With Kade?"

"No." Gabriella turned and grabbed the icing bag she'd prepared. "I mean, not really. We're just so new. Everything is new."

"I don't think it matters how new it is," Chloe said. "You're fated. But I get it. Give it some time. After all, we are talking about Kade here. Luke said he went to Jacksonville."

Gabriella shrugged. She didn't want to talk about it. "He'll be back." She knew that to be true.

"Oh, Ella, I'm sure he'll be home. I mean, of course he will, I'm just—"

"Knock knock."

Both women turned to see the kitchen door swing in as a man walked in. "I hope I'm not interrupting. But I'm looking for Ella," he said. "I'm told she's going to make my dreams come true."

Gabriella's mouth dropped open and she looked to Chloe, who burst into laughter before she got up from her chair. "You've come to the right place," she said to the man. "This is Ella and she's already started making your dreams come true."

Before Gabriella could say anything, Chloe continued. "Ella, this is Grant. He's going to propose to his girlfriend tonight. I'm sorry; I assumed you'd already met."

A giggle bubbled up inside her, but she managed to swallow it down. "Grant." She wiped her hand on her apron quickly before she extended it. "It's nice to meet you. And you're right—I will make your dreams come true, as long as those dreams include a gorgeous cake." She stepped aside to showcase the cake, which still only had a layer of buttercream on it. "It doesn't look like much yet," she said quickly. "But when I'm finished, it will be *delicioso* and *magnifico*. I promise."

"If Ella says it will be perfect," Chloe added, "it will. But you have to tell us, what's the plan? We can't figure it out. Why do you need a cake?"

"I know it's a little unorthodox, but my girlfriend loves cake. I know," he continued when Gabriella and Chloe exchanged glances. "Lots of women love cake. But Sandy *really* loves cake. For me, there was no better way to propose. I'm not sure how much you heard about what I wanted for the cake, but I'm glad to see you haven't started decorating it yet."

She put the icing bag down. "All I was told was a delicious

and beautiful cake. I was going to cover it with flowers in different colors. But if you have a different idea, I'm all ears."

"I like the flower idea," he said. "But I was hoping we could do something a little like this." Grant dug into his back pocket and handed Gabriella a piece of folded paper. The first thought she had when she looked at his plans was one of panic, but it was immediately followed by excitement.

"Do you think you can do it?"

Gabriella nodded and grinned. "I know I can do this."

"Can I see?"

Gabriella tucked the paper against her chest, out of Chloe's sight. "No, *mi amiga*. Not yet."

"You'll see it tonight," Grant said. "I'm going to pop the question after dinner. In front of everyone. Sandy's parents are super important to her and coming on this trip for their thirtieth wedding anniversary was her idea. They need to be there."

"You're going to propose on their wedding anniversary? That's so sweet." Chloe clasped her hand to her chest. "That just seems so romantic. I'm sure she'll love it."

"As long as she says yes."

Gabriella felt tears well up in her eyes. "Something tells me that won't be an issue. It's going to be perfect. Now everyone needs to get out so I can get to work."

He should have said good-bye. Ella would be upset.

It wasn't the first time the thought had crossed his mind. It had been on repeat in his head since he drove out of the garage and down the road. The very last thing he ever wanted to do was upset Ella.

He shook his head. Even thinking that way was evidence of why he needed to make this trip. He wasn't himself. He wasn't acting like himself or making any sense. He'd never been the type of guy to think that way. Ella changed him and so completely. But it had all happened so quickly and instead of being calm and at peace the way a mate was supposed to make him, it had just made him crazier.

Because you're not mated. Axel's voice replayed in his head.

"Dammit." He slammed his hand on the steering wheel and pressed harder on the gas pedal. He didn't want to admit it, but Axel was right. It pissed him off. But he couldn't mate with Ella. He couldn't claim her—even if it was exactly what would save his sanity—knowing what he knew about mating: it would destroy them. And he couldn't let that happen. Not to anyone else he cared about.

Which was exactly why he needed to make this trip. It had been over a year since he'd spoken to his grandfather. Over a year since the Jackson brothers had been cast out of the clan. It was long past time that Kade found out exactly why their grandfather would kick them out for something they hadn't even done. It had been Kira, Kade's twin sister, who'd run off. She'd been the one to go against their grandfather and taken a mate he didn't approve of. They'd done nothing to deserve the treatment they'd received.

Except fail to bring her back.

As he drove, he finally allowed himself to go back to that day in his mind and replay the series of events that had led them to their new life on Grizzly Ridge.

Ryan Dixon was from a grizzly clan in Colorado. The last clan of grizzlies in Colorado. They were known to be very private and had a reputation of being secretive, and some even thought of them as dishonest. A reputation they did nothing to overturn as they successfully hid their existence from the general population, who believed there were no longer any grizzlies left in Colorado. Ryan had been traveling with a group of cousins and friends. The rumor was they'd been on the prowl for suitable females to further their population. As a general rule, bear clans were very hospitable and friendly to travelers. But their grandfather was firm about his dislike for the group and made it clear to all females in the Jackson clan that they weren't to go anywhere near the Dixons, who'd set up a camp just outside of Jackson Valley.

Kira, being the hardheaded female she was, took their grandfather's orders as a challenge and within twelve hours, had snuck out to meet the Dixons and see what all the fuss was about. Of course, she'd been the fuss. And it wasn't even twenty-four hours later that she was gone.

Almost immediately the brothers had been called in for a meeting and told in no uncertain terms that they were to bring Kira home or pay the price for the dishonor brought to her and their clan if they failed.

They'd failed.

The Dixon boys made it as far as Yellowstone before they'd caught up with them. It had been Axel who found them first and convinced Ryan to give them a meeting with Kira. The fact that they had to bargain and barter to talk to their own sister had only pissed Kade off. She was his twin sister, for God's sake. It wasn't right. But if he'd thought that was strange, the meeting was even stranger.

The three brothers sat across from Kira and Ryan, who had his arm wrapped tightly around her, holding her so close to him that it made Kade want to tear his arm off. Of course, every other member of the Dixon clan was there as well. It had felt more like a standoff than a discussion between siblings. The air was thick with tension, and it was clear there would be a battle if the wrong words were uttered by either party.

At any rate, it didn't get that far because Kira hadn't wanted to leave. Being the oldest, Axel had done the talking.

"Kira Jackson," he addressed her, his tone formal and serious, not at all like an older brother who was battling for his little sister's well-being. "We've been sent to bring you home."

"She's not—"

"Let her speak, you—" Luke had to put a hand on Kade's shoulder to shut him up and keep him from charging the man who sat next to his sister. Kade sat back and waited.

When Kira finally spoke, she wouldn't look at him. Her focus was on her oldest brother. "Axel, I appreciate you guys coming down here to find me and I'm sure Grandfather has given you all kinds of orders but..." She held up her hand to stop the protest on Axel's lips. "I'm okay here." She glanced at the man on her left. "More than alright. I'm happy here. This is where I need to be."

"Are you sure?" Axel looked at the men surrounding them, and Kade growled. There was no way Kira was okay. There was no way she would have left without saying good-bye. Her family was everything to her. The four of them were incredibly tight. They'd had to be since their mother and father had left them so young. Especially her and Kade. She wouldn't have left without telling him. Not unless she was forced. It didn't sit right with Kade. Not at all.

He waited on the edge of his seat for her answer. His eyes focused on her, willing her to look his way and speak to him.

She kept her eyes fixed on Axel when she said, "I'm sure."

"You didn't say good-bye." Kade blurted it out before he could be stopped. Luke tried to hold him back again, but he wouldn't be contained. He jumped up from his seat and went to stand in front of his sister. He stopped short of grabbing her and pulling her up in front of him, but only because the man next to her bared his teeth. "Kira, you wouldn't leave like that unless it was—"

"What I *had* to do," she interrupted him. "Kade. I'm sorry."

She stood then, on her own, and grabbed his hand. As she looked him in the eye, he saw right into her soul and the reality hit him in the gut. "Kade, I'm sorry." She squeezed his hand. "I really am. But you know you wouldn't have let me go. There was no other way."

He hated that she was probably right. "I would have," he said. "If it's what you really wanted. Kira, you know I've only ever wanted you to be happy. I wouldn't be able to stand it if you weren't."

Her smile was so sweet, but it didn't quite sparkle the way it usually did. Just remembering the way she looked at him, the smile that was so her, but at the same time...not quite, still made his gut twist.

"I know," she'd said. "But Grandfather wouldn't have let me go." She turned and waved toward their brothers. "You know that. I mean, look. He sent you all to come and get me. I'm a grown woman. I'm more than capable of making my own decisions, but only if it's what he wants. I can't live like that. And he doesn't know Ryan the way I know him."

"Kira." He shook her hands, forcing her to look at him again. "How can you possibly know him? You just met him."

And that was when her face changed and he'd seen it for the first time. *Love.* She was in love with him and there was nothing he'd be able to say. She wouldn't be coming home with them.

"He's my *mate.*"

"No."

"He is, Kade. I know it. I *feel* it."

He looked to Ryan for the first time and immediately wished he hadn't. Kade's fist itched to punch the smirk right off his face. Kade forced himself to look back at Kira to keep himself from doing just that. "Did you....have you..."

She shook her head. "We haven't mated yet."

Kade swallowed hard.

"He says he wants it to be special and—"

"I don't want to hear it."

"If you're not mated, there's still time." Luke appeared at his side and reached for Kira's arm, yanking her toward him. Immediately, the room exploded. The Dixons jumped to attention. Ryan reached for Kira, but not before Luke pulled her behind him.

"Kade," she hissed at him, as if it had been his decision. "Do something."

"Let her go." Ryan stood tall in front of the Jacksons. His arms crossed over his chest, he looked menacing, but Kade had no doubt he could take him. It was the rest of them he wasn't so certain about. Not when there was only three of them against at least a dozen.

"You've not mated her," Luke said. "You have no claim on her."

It was the wrong thing to say. Ryan roared, but in the next moment, the roar faded, and the infernal smirk was back on his face. "I'll claim her right here," he said. "In front of all of you and there won't be a fucking thing you'll be able to do to stop me."

Behind him, Kade heard Kira gasp and a noise something like a sob escaped her. Kira didn't cry.

Looking at the man his twin sister professed to love, and hearing her distress behind him, something in Kade snapped. It was the exact moment he broke. "No." He put a hand on Luke's shoulder before he turned to Axel, who'd make the final call. "No," he said again. Axel looked at him, respect on his face, and stepped to the side, giving Kade the floor again. "There's no need for anyone to get worked up." Each word he spoke broke his heart a little more, but it was what needed to be done. He reached behind him for Kira, who took his hand. He pulled her gently until she stood next to him. "If my sister tells me that she loves you and you're her mate, I won't stop her." She squeezed his hand, but he couldn't look at her. "And neither will my brothers."

"Kade." Her voice was a whisper. A plea for him to look at her. He wouldn't. He couldn't.

Slowly, he extended his arm, with the hand that held Kira's, and offered it to Ryan. "If it's what she wants...she's yours. We won't force her to come with us. But only if it's what she wants."

"It is," she whispered.

Ryan didn't take Kira's hand right away but looked to Axel, the alpha, for affirmation. Kade knew he'd back him up. So would Luke, despite his show. Ultimately, all they wanted was what was best for Kira. No one was going to force her to leave if that's not what was best.

Kade didn't look, but Axel must have nodded and given his consent, because in the next moment, Ryan reached out, took Kira and roughly pulled her toward him, and away from Kade. He still wouldn't look. With a single nod, Kade turned and walked away.

Leaving his sister behind.

Reliving it again, Kade's gut clenched the way it always did when he thought about his sister. He missed her with a physical ache that his brothers couldn't understand. They'd never be able to comprehend what it had been like to walk away from her that day. He'd known it would kill her to leave the man she'd chosen, and he wouldn't do that to her. Even if it meant that walking away from her had killed a part of him.

His bear had died that day. At least as far as he was concerned, it had. It was the bear, the clan, the idea of mating, instincts...everything that was *bear* had caused him to lose the one thing that mattered the most to him: Kira.

He'd vowed then and there that his bear would never again control his future.

But that was before.

Kade navigated his truck down the highway and took the turn that would lead to Jackson Valley.

Before Ella.

Axel and Luke were right; he needed to figure things out. He needed to come to terms with not only his bear, but also the loss of Kira. And he needed to do it before it destroyed him.

The sign said fifty miles to Jacksonville. It would be another fifteen after that to Jackson Valley, where he'd find his grandfather. Kade didn't know what else he hoped to find, but with any luck he'd find at least some of the answers he needed.

CHAPTER EIGHT

"IT'S TIME."

Harper whispered in Gabriella's ear.

"*Si.*" She nodded and gathered up the plates in front of her. "Who's ready for dessert?" She addressed the entire table, which consisted of Grant, his soon-to-be fiancée Sandy, her parents of course, as well as both of Sandy's sisters and their husbands. It had been a nice group to have at the Ridge. Their entire family had filled the guest rooms in the Den and the entire building with laughter, fun, and a sense of family that she'd missed since leaving Argentina.

"Oh, I don't know." Sandy rubbed her stomach. "I'm so full. That was an amazing meal."

"It really was," one of her sisters agreed. "But if dessert is even half as good as that roast was, I definitely want some."

Gabriella smiled and winked. "It's better." She stacked some more plates. "I made a traditional Argentinean *dolche de leche*—"

"Argentinean?" Chloe looked at her with a question. "I thought you were from Peru?"

"Oh, I..." Gabriella stumbled over her words, but recovered

quickly. "I am. But a lot of the recipes transfer and mingle between families." She put on her brightest smile and beamed at Sandy. "It really is the most delicious *dolche de leche* cake you've ever tasted. You simply must try it."

"You had me at cake." She laughed and Gabriella could almost feel the relief wash over Grant, who looked a little more tense as each moment passed. "I never say no to cake."

There was shared laughter around the table while Gabriella escaped to the kitchen. She dropped the dishes by the sink and moved to the walk-in fridge to get the cake she'd only just finished preparing before dinner. It was perfect. Grant had asked her to create figurines for the top. Which she'd done with modeling chocolate. It was a challenge for sure, especially because she didn't have a lot of experience creating figurines. But they'd turned out perfectly. Using a photograph, Gabriella had created the characters to look just like the couple. The little chocolate bride stood on top, dressed in her parka and holding a pair of snowshoes and a mug of hot chocolate. The groom was on one knee, his snowshoes still on his feet, holding out a ring. The actual ring Grant had given Gabriella to include. It was perfect and adorable.

After consulting with Grant, she'd changed her original vision to include only white flowers and cascading ribbons of fondant that made the base of the cake look like snow with the little couple on top. She'd never done anything like it before. Sure, she loved to bake, but she was definitely no cake artist. Or was she?

With a rush of pride, she wished Kade could be there to see what she'd done. But there would be pictures and he'd be back soon. She believed that. She had to.

Gabriella pushed the thoughts of Kade from her head. She needed to focus on the happy couple. It was their day. She'd have hers too. Just not today. With a smile on her face she didn't feel in her heart, Gabriella picked up the cake and headed for the dining room, where everyone was waiting.

"You're going to love this," she called out. "In fact, Sandy, since I know you love cake so much, I'd like you to have the first piece." She made her way around the table, carefully walking in such a way that no one would be able to see the cake until it was time. Just as they'd discussed, Grant met Gabriella and took the cake from her hands. She stepped back to watch as Grant turned carefully and placed the cake in front of his love.

"It's so—"

"Sandy?"

The woman held her hand to her mouth as she realized what was happening and turned to her boyfriend, who was now next to her on one knee.

"Sandy," he started again. "From our first date, I knew there was something special about you and it was our fourth date when I knew without a doubt that I never wanted to spend another day without you." There was a collective sigh from the women around the table. "You make me want to be a better man," Grant continued. "The best version of myself that I can be, for you and with you. We've had some adventures together, but I know it's only just beginning. Sandy..." He reached up and took the ring from the chocolate groom on top of the cake and held it out to her. "Will you make me the happiest man in the world by agreeing to marry me?"

She didn't answer right away, but nodded her head. Slightly at first, and then harder. "Yes," she whispered through her tears. "Yes. Yes. Yes. I will absolutely marry you."

The room erupted in cheers and calls to celebrate. Luke and Chloe appeared with bottles of champagne, which were passed around in a toast to the happy couple. It was the first marriage proposal for Grizzly Ridge, but something told Gabriella, it wouldn't be the last.

Jacksonville looked the same as it had the last time Kade had driven through, little more than a year ago. He wasn't sure why it should have changed in such a short time, but he expected it to look different considering *he* felt so different. If anything, the shops looked smaller, more run-down than they used to. The streets he'd run around in as a teenager now seemed too small to contain him.

Funny how things could change so quickly.

He contemplated stopping in for a pint at the Growl, but thought better of it. With the mood he was in, one pint could easily turn into two, which could roll into three. And if his grandfather smelled even a whiff of beer on him, the conversation might be over before it began. Considering he didn't even know what he was going to say, nothing good could come out of that.

Instead, he drove past the same regular trucks and rusted-out cars parked out front that had always been there. He shook his head, and steered off the main road to the gravel trail that would lead him up to Jackson Valley.

The valley was only about fifteen minutes out of town, but it might as well have been a world away. It was both considered a part of town, and yet a little village of its own. Besides the main house where Kade and his brothers grew up, there were a number of trailers scattered around the property that had been hauled up over the years and housed mostly single bears who worked in town at the mill. There were a few families, but after the Jackson cubs had grown up, there were less and less children around. When they were young, it had been the perfect place to grow up. After school, they'd run off the bus and spend the rest of the afternoon climbing trees, running with their bears and just generally getting into trouble. It had been great. But then everything changed.

He pulled up in front of the house, next to his grandfather's truck. He hadn't doubted that he would find him at home. He still owned the Jackson mill, but he hadn't spent a day working there for years. All three brothers had been given jobs when they graduated from high school, and Axel had been in line to take over and run it. No doubt one of their cousins was now in place to do just that. There was a time that would have bothered Kade, but the mill business had never been his dream. And now that they had Grizzly Ridge, he was even more sure of that.

That's what he wanted—a life at the Ridge.

No.

A life at the Ridge with Ella.

That's what he wanted.

And with that thought in his head, he slammed the door of his truck and made his way up the steps of his childhood home. He knocked, but there was no doubt his grandfather already knew he was there.

He waited. And waited. But he wasn't in a hurry.

He'd wait.

At least five minutes went by before he finally heard the steps inside, followed by the turning of the handle. When the heavy wooden door swung open, Kade stepped to the side.

The man who stood in front of him was still the same strong force of a man he'd known, but this version of his grandfather was old. He had an edge about him that radiated. The anger and unhappiness that flowed from him had never been there before and it assaulted Kade's instincts. Sure, their grandfather had been tough, but he'd always been a fair man. Despite their mother and father leaving them, none of the Jackson kids had ever felt unloved.

The man who stood before him now was different. If Kade

hadn't been so angry with him, he might have felt some sympathy. As it was, Kade closed his heart to that instinct. He needed to stay focused.

"Kade."

"Grandfather."

They stared at each other for a moment, each of them waiting for the other to make the first move. Despite his decision not to, Kade couldn't help but let some emotion sneak in. After all, this was the man who'd raised them.

He's also the man who banished you.

Kade swallowed hard and held his ground.

"You look well," Grandfather said after a moment.

"As do you." Kade nodded and then shook his head. "No. You look—"

"Old?"

He couldn't help but crack a smile. "Yes. You look old."

"Life will do that to you." There was no humor in his voice. "I suppose you would like to come in."

He didn't wait for an answer but turned and led the way into the living room. Kade followed. His eyes took in the house as he walked down the hallway. Everything was exactly the same as when they'd left. Nothing had changed.

Nothing.

School portraits of all four kids lined the hallway; a thick layer of dust covered their edges. Kade resisted the urge to wipe his finger along the top of the frames. The living room was musty. The curtains were drawn, allowing only slivers of light in the cracks. Dust motes danced in the dim light. It was a good thing the curtains were closed, Kade thought, or the dust would be even more noticeable. It had been one of their chores, to clean the inside of the house. Surely he must have had someone else come in and clean since they'd been gone?

But it certainly didn't look like it.

Grandfather gestured to the couch before he sat in his recliner. It was the only part of the room that looked lived in. As Kade sat, dust billowed up and into his nostrils from the cushions. He ignored it.

"I'm surprised it took you so long to come see me." His grandfather was never one for small talk, but even then, Kade hadn't been prepared for such a direct approach. "I expected you months ago."

"I didn't see any point."

"And now you do."

It wasn't a question, but Kade answered it as one. "I do. I need answers, Grandfather."

He nodded.

"Will you give them to me?"

"I'll tell you what you want to know. But it's not what you're looking for."

CHAPTER NINE

HOW DID he know what Kade was looking for? The idea that the old man could be so presumptuous ignited a rage in him, but he quickly swallowed it down. It wouldn't do any good to get confrontational with him. Not if he wanted to know the truth.

"What is it you want to know, Kade?"

"Why?" he asked instinctually.

It was such a vague question, it could have meant anything but Gordon knew at once what his grandson meant.

"Because that's how things are done," Gordon answered. "What you don't understand, Kade, is that everything we do, our traditions...everything is done for a reason. To protect the clan."

"How does casting us out protect us?" He hadn't meant to fire off with emotion, but if Grandfather noticed, he didn't say anything.

"It's the alpha's job to create and maintain order among the clan. That's what I did."

"That's not what you did!"

"It is, Kade. I gave you an order and you didn't obey it. I had no other choice."

Kade could see the pain in the old man's eyes as he spoke the words. It had cost him to cast out his grandchildren. But he couldn't spare the sympathy.

"There's always a choice." Kade leaned forward in his seat and rested his elbows on his knees. "What you don't know, Grandfather, is that there's no way we could have done what you asked. Even if Kira hadn't been surrounded by another clan who was ready for a fight, we never would have made her come with us. Not if she didn't want to. And she didn't. She found her mate."

"No, Kade. She didn't."

The words slammed into him, into the little sliver of doubt he'd held onto since that moment he'd turned his back and walked away from his twin. He dropped his head and looked at his hands clenched between his legs. He couldn't let his grandfather get to him.

"I know she did, Grandfather." He was lying, mostly to himself, but he had to continue. "Because Kira looked at him the way I now look at my mate."

The second the words were out of his mouth, he knew it to be true. Ella was his mate. It had never felt more right. And he'd tell her so as soon as he got home, but first he needed to deal with things. He couldn't move forward until he'd put the past behind him. That had never been as clear as it was right at that moment. He closed his eyes and leaned his head back on the couch, giving himself a moment to process the realization. When he opened his eyes again, his grandfather was smiling.

"So, it's finally happened, has it? You've found yourself a mate?"

Kade nodded, not trusting himself to speak for the moment.

"I'd heard that your brothers had found themselves matches as well. I worried about you, though, Kade."

"You did?"

"Of course. You were the youngest when you lost your mother. Well, you and Kira of course. And then there was everything with your sister." He took a deep breath as if it pained him to talk about it. Even if it did, Kade was going to make him say everything he needed to. "I was worried it might have damaged you."

It did. He wanted to scream at his grandfather. He wanted to let him know the hell he'd gone through, was still going through, all because of the decisions he'd made around his mother and sister. "I know why you banished us," he said instead. "Tell me why you banished my mother. You never talked about it."

"It's not something you talk about. As an alpha, it's—"

"I don't care." Kade had had enough. "You can't cover this with alpha bullshit, Grandfather. She's your daughter, our mother. That's what matters. You cast her out. We grew up without a mother and a father because of you. Tell me what happened. I deserve at least that much."

The old man rubbed his temples, looking every one of his eighty-two years. When they were growing up, Kade had always thought of him as invincible. There was nothing he couldn't do. Larger than life, in control of every situation. That man was gone. Whatever was left of the grandfather he knew had disappeared with Kade's demand.

"You're right," he said after a moment. "You do deserve to know. But I'm afraid any answer I give you won't be enough."

"Try me."

There was a pause and then a deep sigh. "I know you don't want to hear it, but the truth was very simple. Like your sister, Tonia fell in love with someone she shouldn't have."

"Her mate, you mean."

Gordon shrugged. "It didn't matter. She was promised in a very careful arrangement with a clan from Alaska."

"Alaska?"

He nodded. "You have to understand that it was important to build relations with other clans and create arrangements that would benefit our bloodline."

"But Mom had other plans."

"She did." Gordon's face took on a faraway look. "She was always a strong-willed girl. She knew what she wanted. Just like her brothers."

His grandfather didn't mention Kade's uncles very often. There'd been an accident at the mill when he was young. Brian, the oldest brother, had been killed; Spencer had lost a leg and hadn't adapted to his new circumstances well. He'd never married and as far as Kade knew, still lived in a trailer at the edge of the property. Alone. "I told her if she chose Mark, she was choosing his clan and she wouldn't be welcome back in Jackson Valley."

"And that's what she chose."

The old man nodded slowly. "It was a decision I had to make as the—"

"Alpha," Kade finished for him with a shake of his head.

"But as a father it broke my heart." There was a catch in his voice Kade had never heard before. "I had no other choice, Kade. If I'd allowed it, I would have lost the respect of the clan. There would have been mutiny. I couldn't risk it."

"But she came back."

"She did. And I'll never forget that day. Your father was sick; she asked me for help with you cubs. She didn't want you to see your father die." The words hit Kade like a blow. *Die. His father was dead?* He didn't know his dad, had been little more than a toddler when they'd gone to live in Jackson Valley, but still the knowledge hurt. He swallowed it down and kept listening. "I'm not proud of what happened that day, Kade. I gave her a choice. I told her I'd take in you cubs, but if she wanted to return to the clan, she'd have to do so with you, and without him."

"And leave her mate to die alone." The choice seemed unfathomable.

Gordon nodded and said simply, "She chose him."

When their guests were done celebrating, they all retreated to their rooms and some to the outdoor hot tub the brothers had recently installed to have another glass of champagne, Luke and Axel offered to clean up in the kitchen. It was an offer all three women happily accepted as they crashed on the couch in front of the fireplace. It was quickly becoming Gabriella's favorite place to sit and decompress. Especially with the other women. She'd never had friends like Chloe and Harper. These women didn't know she was the daughter of the alpha and set to be in a position of power in the clan, and they liked her anyway. Maybe they liked her because they didn't know. Would they think the same of her when they knew the truth?

Gabriella looked at Chloe, who flipped through some sort of notebook and jotted things down occasionally, and Harper, who was knitting what looked to be like a baby blanket. She tried not to giggle, because Harper didn't seem like the type of woman who would be knitting, but then again, having a baby did strange things to a person. They looked so comfortable and *real*. She took a deep breath.

Yes. They'd still like her.

And it was long past time to tell them the truth.

She settled herself into the seat closest to the fire, the one she sat in on her first day at the Ridge. The one she'd come to think of as her own.

"It's about time you sat down, Ella." Chloe glanced up from

her notebook. "If the guys want to clean up, that's never something I question." She laughed and tucked her book away. "Besides, you worked so hard in there today. That cake was amazing."

"It really was. I had no idea you could do that kind of decorating."

"Neither did I," Gabriella answered Harper. "I think I'm learning that I'm capable of a lot more than I thought I was." She took a deep breath. "In fact, I've been learning a lot ever since I left Argentina."

"Argentina?" Chloe caught it the way Gabriella knew she would.

She nodded.

"I thought you said you were from Peru?"

She took another deep breath. "I did. I lied."

"Why?" Harper put down her knitting. "Why would you lie?"

The hurt in the other woman's voice stung. "I didn't think I had a choice," she started. "But I know now that I do, so I'm hoping I can tell you the truth and you'll keep an open mind."

Harper opened her mouth to say something, but it was Chloe who answered. "Of course. I don't know what you're hiding, Ella. But from what we know of you, there must have been a reason you did it. Besides, you're Kade's mate and that definitely counts for a lot."

She flinched at the mention of Kade again. She hadn't heard from him all day and if his brothers knew anything, they weren't saying. "Well, all that aside, there is a reason I lied. I'm not proud of it, but I think you'll understand." She forced a smile. "I *hope* you'll understand."

"Ella." Harper's smile was warm. "Of course we'll—"

"That's the first thing." She might as well jump in. "My name isn't Ella Rodriguez. Well, not really." At their confused expressions, she continued. "My full name is Gabriella Santos. Ella was the nickname my *abuela* gave me and Rodriguez was my mother's surname."

"I don't understand." Chloe shook her head. "Why would you tell us a fake name? It doesn't make any sense."

"But it does." Gabriella shifted in the chair and wrung her hands together. "You see, I took this job and came here to escape. I couldn't use my name. I needed to—"

"Escape?"

"Oh!" Harper grabbed her stomach. The other women looked at her in concern, but she nodded and gestured Gabriella to continue.

"It's not the same there as it is here. My father is the alpha of our clan and he's very strict. I was promised to a bear when I was born. You see, we're almost extinct and it's crucial for our bloodline to continue, so he—"

"Oh! Ow!" This time when Harper cried out, neither Chloe nor Gabriella could ignore it. She bent over, her arms wrapped around her stomach.

"Harper. What's wrong?" Chloe was on her knees next to her friend in seconds. She looked up to Gabriella. "Go get Axel. Now. Something's not right."

———

His grandfather had been right. He may now know the truth, but it still wasn't what he needed to know. The problem was, Kade didn't know what it was he *needed* to know. He'd excused himself to the bathroom to gather his thoughts, but he couldn't put it off any longer. He needed to put an end to the visit.

Gordon called him out the second he returned to the living room. "Why did you come, Kade?"

"I told you. For answers."

"And did you get them?"

He shook his head. "No."

They sat in silence for a moment before his grandfather said, "Tell me about her."

"Ella?"

"That's her name? It's pretty. I imagine she is as well."

It felt both strange and comfortable talking to his grandfather about Ella. It wasn't that long ago that they were a family and despite everything that he'd done—the choices he'd made, the rifts created—he was still family. Kade sighed and a smile came to his face the way it always did when he thought of Ella. "She's gorgeous. And before you ask, she's not from here so you likely don't know her clan. She's a bespectacled bear."

"Bespectacled? Really?" An expression Kade couldn't quite read crossed his grandfather's face, but it was gone so fast he couldn't be sure he saw it. "It's been a long time since I've come across a bespectacled bear. She must be from..."

"Peru."

"Peru? Really?"

"Yes." Kade paused for a moment before he continued. "She came to work for us at the Ridge. She's a wonder in the kitchen and..."

"And your mate?"

"Yes. Well, not officially. I mean, we haven't...I haven't..."

"You haven't claimed her yet."

"No."

"Can I ask why not?"

Kade thought on it for a moment and decided on the truth. "I needed answers from you first," he said.

"About your mother?"

"Yes." He nodded. "And Kira." He walked to the bookshelf where family pictures had always been displayed. His eyes landed on his favorite one: a picture of Kade and Kira about sixteen years old. Young enough to dream big and naive enough to believe those dreams would come true.

"You said you didn't get the answers you were looking for."

Kade didn't turn around, but kept his eyes fixed on the picture. He remembered what his grandfather had said about Kira not finding her mate. The worry came back, but he quickly dismissed it. If she'd been unhappy, she would have come home. Kira knew he'd always be there for her. Besides, if she was in any kind of distress, he would have sensed it. The connection between twins was strong. Especially in bears.

But you've denied your bear. Kira's voice rang in his head.

He *had* denied his bear. And for what? His mate had found him anyway. Besides that, it was all of a sudden clear to him that it wasn't mates or mating that was the problem. It wasn't the idea of a fated mate, or choosing a mate that ripped families apart.

It was his grandfather.

Once the idea took root, he couldn't understand why he hadn't seen it all along. He'd denied his bear for so long for all the wrong reasons. He was punishing himself for something that wasn't his fault.

"I was wrong," he said slowly. "I did get the answers I was looking for." He turned around slowly and looked his grandfather straight in the eye. "I know now I was wrong. All this time, it was you. It was always you."

"It was me, what?"

"You're the one who tore this family apart. It was all you."

"Kade, it—"

"It was you," he said again. "Years ago, you made a choice with my mother and you made another with Kira."

Gordon opened his mouth, but Kade wasn't ready to let him talk. "I can see the toll it's taken on you, and despite everything you've done, I feel bad for you." He realized it was true. "But I can't fix it for you." He crossed the room, ready to leave. He got what he'd come for. "Only you can fix this, Grandfather." He paused and turned around. "But only if you want to. And you know what else I know now?"

The old man, who'd seemed to have aged even further in the last few moments, shook his head.

"When it comes to my life, no matter what you've done, I'm the one in charge. It's about time I realized that."

Kade didn't wait for a response. He turned, walked out of his childhood home, and didn't look back. He was focused, and the object of that focus—Ella. His mate.

CHAPTER TEN

IT WAS late before Gabriella finally closed up the Den and went up to Kade's cabin to retire for the night. She'd been determined to wait up for word of Harper and how she was doing. Chloe and Luke had accompanied Harper and Axel down the mountain to the hospital, and hadn't returned until after midnight. Harper was stable. They'd done an ultrasound and the baby looked fine.

For now.

Her blood pressure was too high and the doctors wanted to keep her in the hospital for a few days to monitor her. It was complicated, of course, by the fact that the baby Harper was carrying was no ordinary baby, but the doctors didn't know that. Gabriella had never heard of a half-blood shifter carrying a baby to term, let alone getting pregnant. It was definitely a pregnancy that was rife with complications. She said a silent prayer for Harper and the cub as she stood on the porch and looked up to the stars before she walked through the door of the cabin she'd already started to think of as hers as well as Kade's.

But it felt different without Kade there to warm it up. And warm her up. The winter nights were cold. She didn't think she'd ever get used to that part of living in Montana. It was bearable with Kade snuggled up to her, his strong, muscular body pressed against her back, his arm holding her tight to him as if he'd never let her go.

But he had let go.

The little voice in the back of her head that she'd been trying so hard to push away all day finally snuck in as she changed into the warmest pajamas she could find. It was a pair Chloe had lent her, although she hadn't worn them yet. There was no need with her big natural furnace keeping her hot every night. Very hot. But he wasn't there now. He'd left. And as much as she knew it wasn't about her—well, not really—she couldn't help but feel that it actually had everything to do with her.

Gabriella crawled under the thick blankets and tucked them as tightly as she could around her shivering body. Despite everything, she was exhausted. Within seconds, her eyes drifted shut and she fell into a solid sleep.

It may have been cold outside, but Gabriella's dreams were anything but. Kade was there. Curled up behind her, his body pressed hard up against her, he heated her through her flannel pajamas. One hand slipped around her waist, his fingers playing with the elastic waistband of her pants. "I don't like these," Kade growled in her ear before he bit down gently on her lobe. "I like you naked in my bed."

Gabriella moaned and wriggled up against dream Kade.

His lips and tongue continued to lavish attention on the sensitive spot behind and just beneath her earlobe while his hand abandoned the waistband to slip under her top. He splayed his fingers over her belly and pulled her closer to him. She could have sworn she could have felt the thick pulse of his erection against her back, even in her dream.

"You feel so damn good." Kade's hand moved up to her

breast, where he pinched and flicked her nipple until it was a hard, throbbing peak, desperate for more attention. She tried to turn her head, needing more, but when his hand once again moved down to her waistband, before slipping beneath it, she couldn't focus on the kiss she so desperately wanted only seconds before.

"These pants have got to go." With a quick move, Kade tugged her pants down around her knees and in the next instant, his fingers found her heat between her legs. Even in her dreams, she was so ready for him. Her body always wanted him. Even in sleep. And with him gone, she'd take what she could get. When he was once again wrapped behind her, Gabriella ground her bottom into him, eliciting a groan of pleasure from him. "God, I want you right now," he murmured in her ear.

"Take me, Kade. Please. I need you here." She spoke aloud, surprising herself. Gabriella's eyes popped open, destroying her dream.

Only it hadn't destroyed her dream at all.

Before Gabriella had time to make sense of what was going on, there was a shift behind her. Kade's hand gripped her hip, lifting her slightly, and then his hard, hot length slid between her legs and inside her.

Damn, she felt good. But that wasn't enough to really explain how it felt to be inside Ella. She gasped when he entered her and twisted around, her eyes wide with surprise.

"Sorry to wake you, baby." He grinned mischievously and thrust his hips.

"I thought I was dreaming."

"Every day with you is a dream." It was one of the cheesier

things he'd said, but it was exactly how he felt and he was tired of hiding it. "Nice way to wake up?"

"The best." She smiled and turned her head around, pressing it against him so they were curled together perfectly.

He kept his hand on her hip and moved her back as he moved forward, slowly moving inside her. She moaned. Just loud enough for him to hear. He kept up his rhythm as he left a trail of kisses on the back of her neck, and just below the collar of the ridiculous pajamas she wore. His lips lingered on the base of her neck. He could claim her now.

He *should* claim her now.

They'd be mated before morning. Just the way he knew she wanted to be. The way he now knew he wanted them to be.

As if she'd sensed what he was contemplating, Ella shifted in his grip. "No," she said. "Not now. Tonight I just want to feel you."

He hesitated. There was no point in waiting, but if she didn't want to go ahead, for whatever reason, he'd wait. He'd never do anything she didn't want. Not ever.

"Okay," he said after a moment. "Then tonight, you'll feel." He shifted focus immediately, and moved his hand between her legs again to the throbbing bundle of nerves he found there. He knew exactly what would make her crazy, and with a few well-timed gentle pinches, Ella squirmed under his ministrations. It didn't take him long to bring her to climax. The feeling of her losing control around him was almost too much for him, but he wasn't done yet.

He waited until Ella's quivers slowed before he slipped out of her and turned her on her back. An instant later, he was on top of her, looking into her beautiful eyes.

"I wanted to see you. No. I *needed* to see you, Ella."

Once again, he plunged inside her and as he did, her face twisted into a smile of pleasure. She responded so readily to him. They'd been born to fit together. He'd never felt about anyone the way he felt about Ella. Everything she was was pure and honest and...true. And she was his.

She reached up and pulled him down to her lips, kissing him hard. "I'm glad you're home," she said against his lips. "Don't leave again."

"Never." The promised slipped out, but he meant it.

Kade thrust harder, and then again. He felt the familiar tightening of her body as Ella once again reached her climax, and this time, looking in her eyes, he went over the edge with her.

She'd said no to him. He wanted to claim her; Gabriella had sensed it. And she'd said no.

Sexually satisfied, the rest of her pajamas discarded on the floor, she was wrapped in his arms, her head on his chest, and she finally had a moment to think about what she'd done.

They could have been mated and she would be tied to him forever. Safe from any threat of returning to Argentina and Carlos. It's what she wanted, what she'd been waiting for him to be ready for. But now things had changed. She couldn't mate Kade. Not without her telling him the truth. He deserved to know who she really was and where she was really from. He deserved the truth.

"Kade?" She propped herself up on her elbow and stared at his handsome face. It was lined with exhaustion, his eyes closed, but she knew he wasn't asleep. Not quite. "I need to tell you something."

"Mmhm."

"Are you asleep?"

"Mmmmm."

"Can we talk?"

His eyes fluttered open and his arm squeezed her shoulders. "Of course," he said, his voice thick with sleep. "But can we talk in the morning? I have a lot I need to tell you, too."

"Of course." She forced a smile. She'd been so focused on what she needed to tell him she'd momentarily forgotten that of course he would have a lot to tell her, too. And she both wanted and needed to hear what he had to say. Because wherever he'd run off to without an explanation had clearly changed things for him. She could feel the shift in him. "Let's talk tomorrow."

He nodded and his eyes closed again.

"Oh, and Kade?"

"Mmmmm?"

"I'm really glad you came back and I would really like to…"

"I know, baby," he murmured. He opened his eyes and pulled her over to him to give her a thorough kiss. "Now get some sleep."

CHAPTER ELEVEN

"WHAT DO YOU THINK?" Gabriella asked him again. She knew she was pushing her luck but she also knew that Kade had to be almost ready to explore his bear. Finally. Something was different about him now. He was different. "It's a beautiful morning." She glanced out the window and winced. "Well, for a winter morning, it's a beautiful morning."

He wrapped his arms around her and pulled her back down into bed with him. "You know what's beautiful?" He rolled on top of her. One arm braced him so he hovered right above her; his other hand cupped her face and stroked her cheek with his thumb. "You."

There was no way she was going to let him get away from it that easily. She rolled to the side. "And it's beautiful outside." She was lying through her teeth. It looked seriously cold, but she was getting used to it. A little. "Let's go for a run. Come on, it'll be fun."

He hesitated for a moment and it gave her hope.

"Besides," she continued to push. "It'll give us time to be alone." She definitely needed to be alone with him. She had a lot to tell him still, but selfishly, shifting and going for a run would be just the stress release she needed before such a conversation. It could only help both of them.

"We can be alone here." He rolled her back toward him so she was under him again. He kissed her and it was almost enough to change her mind. Almost.

"Kade, come on."

Before he could object again, she jumped out of bed. Naked, she walked backward to the front room, her crooked finger beckoning him as she went. "It'll be fun. I need this. And I think you need this."

Just as she knew he would, Kade got out of bed and followed her.

Watching him walk toward her took her breath away. He was a magnificent man. In every way.

"What's that tattoo for?" When he got close enough, she trailed her fingers down his arm and the tattoo that covered it.

"Come back to bed and I'll tell you."

Gabriella's smile was sweet, but there was steel behind it. "I'll make you a deal. If you tell me, I'll tell you a secret." She was playing with fire. Her secrets weren't bargaining chips to be negotiated with. "But first...let's run."

"No." He shook his head, and she could see the resolution in his face this time. "I'm not ready. But I'm ready to talk." He took her hand gently and led her back toward the bedroom. "I went to see my grandfather yesterday."

She nodded.

"It changed everything, Ella. I know you want to mate."

"Only if you—"

"I do." He took her face in his hands, holding her fast so she couldn't look away. "You have to know that's what I've wanted from the moment I met you. Maybe even before." He nodded to himself. "Yes, definitely it was even before I'd even met you. But I couldn't."

"Why?"

"I can't even explain it so it'll make sense, but there's a lot of history with my family."

"Chloe and Harper told me some of it."

His thumb stroked her cheek slowly as he spoke, but he still held her firm, looking directly into her eyes. "I'm sure Luke and Axel filled them in, but there's probably more they don't know. But it doesn't matter. The short version is, I blamed my bear for...well, for everything."

"And now?"

"Now I don't. Now I know it's part of me. Just the way you're part of me. I believe that now. No." He paused. "I *know* that now. You're part of me and you have been the moment I sensed you out there on the road. Probably before. After all, there's a reason you left Peru and came here to us. To me. It was fate."

Gabriella swallowed hard. She wanted to believe like he did that it was fate. And maybe it was, but it was also something more. Something he still needed to know. "Kade, I need to tell—"

The shrill ring of his cell phone cut her off.

"Ignore it," she said. He glanced over at it. "Please." Instinctually, she knew what it was and they couldn't ignore it. Harper was still in the hospital and Kade didn't even know that yet. Something could be wrong with her. Something could be really wrong. She was being selfish and she knew it.

"It's Luke."

She was about to tell Kade it could wait, but she would never be able to live with herself if something happened. "Answer it. A lot happened yesterday. It'll be important."

"Harper's in the hospital?"

They were sitting in the Den and Kade's mind was spinning with the news about his brother's mate. Sure, he'd objected to her when she'd first arrived at the Ridge, but he could admit when he was wrong, and he'd been wrong about Harper. He'd grown to love her like a sister.

No.

Not like Kira.

But still, he loved her and the news that she was in the hospital with complications from her pregnancy hit him hard.

"How come you didn't tell me?" He turned to Ella, who sat next to him.

"I didn't really have a chance." It was true, but she still looked as if she was hiding something. *What else hadn't she told him?* She'd mentioned something...there wasn't time to think about it.

"What can we do?" Kade turned his attention back to Luke and Chloe. "There must be something we can do."

Chloe shook her head. "I spoke to Axel earlier. She's stable but her blood pressure is really high. Too high. They're monitoring her but she'll have to stay in the hospital for a few more days at least. I canceled my work trip, so I'll stick around and help here."

"*Dios mio.*"

Kade reached over and grabbed Ella's hand, giving it a squeeze. "She'll be okay." He looked at Chloe again. "Won't she?"

It was Luke who answered. "Carrying a cub is hard work. And she's only half bear."

Ella shook her head in disagreement with what Luke was implying. "She's strong enough."

Kade nodded. "Ella's right. She's strong enough."

"Ella?" Chloe raised her eyebrows and looked pointedly at his mate. "You haven't told him anything?"

He glanced between the two women. Ella turned away, but not quick enough that he couldn't see the look of panic on her face. "Tell me what?"

"There hasn't really been a chance." She spoke to Chloe. "And I still need to explain things to you as well."

"I know we got a little interrupted yesterday." Chloe's face was kind. "And I'm sure there's a good explanation for everything. But I kind of think that maybe Kade should know first."

"What?" He grew impatient. "What do I need to know first?"

Ella turned to him and took his hands. The look on her face worried him, though. Her smile was gone. "There's something I need to tell you."

"Clearly." He didn't want to be short with her, but his bear bristled. His instincts, as muted as they were, were on high alert. Something wasn't right and he couldn't be sure, given the state of his bear at the moment, but it was more than whatever secret Ella had to tell him.

"Can we go somewhere and talk?"

"Tell me here."

She glanced nervously at Chloe and Luke.

"Sounds like they already know something I don't," he said, trying to push his bear down. Getting angry before he had a reason to wouldn't help anything. "Might as well talk right here."

"I don't know anything, man." Luke shrugged and wrapped his arm around Chloe. "Besides, we're leaving. Since Axel and Harper are down in town, and our guests are checking out this morning, I convinced my beautiful mate here to take the snowmobiles out. With any luck, we'll be gone for the day."

"That'll give you lots of time to talk," Chloe added.

"And it'll give us lots of time to—"

Chloe smacked Luke's arm to shut him up before she dragged him out of the room, leaving Kade alone with Ella and whatever secrets she had to share.

As soon as they were gone, Kade stood and walked to the window. Something wasn't right. He couldn't shake the feeling. He looked out at the parking lot area but the only people out there were the guests loading up their cars. He craned his neck to look farther down the road. But there was nothing. It had been snowing when he got in the night before, but Luke must have plowed the road while he'd been sleeping in. Nothing looked out of place.

"Kade..."

He took one more look outside. His instincts were way off. They'd been foggy for too long. He must be picking up on whatever was going on with Ella.

"Please come sit down with me. *Por favor*. There's something I need to tell you. Please don't be angry."

He took a deep breath and exhaled slowly. He couldn't be angry with her. After all, he had secrets, too. "I'm not angry." He turned and walked across the room to her. He took her hand in his and sat next to her on the overstuffed leather couch. "And you're not the only one with secrets. Would it be okay if I went first?"

She nodded the way he hoped she would.

"Please know I never intended to hide anything about myself from you," he started. "In fact, most of what I'm going to tell you happened long before I met you. But I hope it helps you understand why I've been so hesitant when it comes to us."

"Kade, you don't have to explain."

"I do. Because I love you, you and I are fated and more than anything, I want you and me to be mated. But first you need to understand. And then whatever you have to tell me, I'll be ready to hear that. There's nothing we can't face together. Okay?"

"*Si*." She nodded, and her beautiful smile reassured him that of course, everything would be okay. "*Te amo*, Kade."

Over the next two hours, Kade filled Ella in on everything that had happened with his mother, his sister, his visit to his grandfather, and most importantly, the realizations he'd come to. By the time he had finished telling her everything, they were both exhausted.

"Are you...do you..."

"I'm fine," she said. "More than fine because now I understand everything." She leaned over and kissed him hard. The kind of kiss that made everything okay. More than okay. He wrapped his arms around her and pulled her on to his lap so she straddled him.

"I'd say you're fine." It was cheesy but more than appropriate at that moment. He was done talking. At least for the moment. All he needed was his woman. And he needed her with a ferocity that would not be ignored and was currently pressing into her. Hard.

She still hadn't told him what she needed to, and it would be so easy to ignore that fact considering Kade was currently kissing her as if his life depended on it. But she couldn't ignore it. She had to tell him the truth.

Reluctantly, Gabriella pulled back so she could look into his eyes. "I still need to tell you—"

He moved his attentions to her neck and kissed and suckled his way down to the v of her shirt. "It can wait."

Maybe it could wait. If he kept kissing her the way he was, it most definitely could wait.

No.

She shook her head.

"Kade, it can't. I need to tell you—"

"Oh, I think it can." His fingers tugged at the buttons of her shirt and revealed the swell of her breasts, were he started to lavish attention.

For a moment, Gabriella sank into the sensation. *Damn, he was good at distracting her. Too good.*

"My name isn't Ella." She blurted it out before she could change her mind or be distracted by something else. Kade's mouth froze, his lips poised over her breast. He held the position for so long she started to wonder whether he was okay. "Kade?"

Slowly, Kade sat up so he looked in her eyes again. She could see the swirl of emotions roiling through him. He was confused, but something else as well.

"What did you say?"

She swallowed hard, but sat up straight as she repeated herself. "My name isn't Ella." She paused long enough for that to sink in before she added, "It's Gabriella. Gabriella Santos. Ella is a nickname I haven't used since I was a child. And Rodriguez was my mother's maiden name. She died when I was a child. I grew up with my father, and my *abuela*, in our clan..." She took another deep breath. "In Argentina."

"You're from Peru."

"No." She shook her head. "My name is Gabriella Santos and I'm from the Santos clan in Argentina."

She couldn't read his expression. Where only a second ago it had been warm and open, with only a few words Kade had closed off. Closed her out. "Say something. *Por favor*, Kade."

"Who are you?" He shook his head slowly, his body stiff under hers.

She clenched her thighs around him, needing to hold on. Needing to be connected. "I'm still me. I'm still Ella. Everything about us is true. It's real. We're real."

"How can that be? You lied about who you were."

"I had no choice." Tears sprang to her eyes and she didn't bother to wipe them away. She hadn't allowed herself to cry in a long time. There was no point. Tears did nothing. They got her nowhere. Even when she'd gone to her father in tears because Carlos had hit her that first time—nothing.

Her father had looked at her, his normally warm eyes full of love turned to ice. "That's what men do, Gabriella. You must learn to obey."

Reeling, she'd left her father's office that day and gone home. She'd hidden in her room for two days before the bruises had faded enough to cover them with makeup. Two days before she went out in public and faced Carlos once again. He'd sworn he'd never hit her again. He'd sworn he'd never hurt her. But that was just the beginning.

How could she tell Kade all of that? Tell him that the woman he'd fallen in love with had been too weak to stand up for herself? Too scared to leave sooner or just say no to the whole marriage? She shook her head. She couldn't.

"You always have a choice, Ella. Gabriella. Whatever." He turned away and it almost killed her.

"Kade." She touched his cheek, forcing him to turn and look at her. "I'm still the same Ella. I don't know if I can make you understand. But I think…" An idea came to her. "It's not all that different from Kira or your mother."

His face twisted into a scowl and he shook his head. "Don't—"

"Kade Jackson." Gabriella grabbed his face with both hands and forced him to look her in the eyes. "Don't look away from me. I won't let you. Look me in the eyes and tell me you don't see how much I love you."

"Ella...this is—"

"Do it."

He did and immediately Gabriella could see the love reflected in his eyes. Despite the hurt and confusion, there was love there; she could see it. He might be angry and confused. But he loved her. Of that there was no doubt.

"Now, you listen to me," she said as firmly as she could. "And don't say one word until I'm done. Then you can decide if I'm telling the truth or not. Then you decide if you want to be with me or not."

CHAPTER TWELVE

OF COURSE he wanted to be with her. His entire body vibrated with his need for her. He wanted nothing more than to make her his. He knew that more than ever now. Or, at least he thought he had.

Confusion clouded his head. She'd lied. Everything she'd said was a lie. Everything he knew about her.

She wasn't Ella?

She wasn't from Peru?

Who was she?

He looked at her. Really looked at her. Took his time taking in her round hips, the curve of her waist, the swell of her breasts, up to her golden eyes, currently fixed on him waiting for him to respond.

She'd fixed him with her stare and wanted him to listen.

But he couldn't.

Not yet.

"Kade, I need you to hear me. *Por favor*. Listen."

He clenched his jaw.

"I had to lie," she started. "You don't understand how it was for me. My father, he's the alpha of our clan and much like what it must have been like for your sister, he decided who I would mate with, for the betterment of the clan."

"And you fell in love with someone else and ran off." His words came out harsher than intended. If she was really so much like his sister, that's exactly what had happened.

"What?" She shook her head. "No. I mean, yes. I did fall in love with someone else, but not until later. Not until I got here."

It took him a moment to realize she was talking about him.

"But I did run," she continued before he could respond. "I had to."

"No." He shook his head. "You didn't have to run. There is always a choice. Just like my mother had a choice, Kira had a choice, and my grandfather did, too. You had a choice, Ella. And you chose to run."

He couldn't do it. He wanted to hear what she had to say. More than anything, he wanted an explanation for why she lied. An explanation that would make it all okay. But he knew it wouldn't be fair to hear it right now. He wouldn't be able to listen. Not fairly. His bear was right at the surface, in a way it hadn't been in years. He was way too on edge to have a conversation that could affect his entire life and he didn't want to say or do anything he'd regret. That wouldn't be fair to either of them.

Kade could see the hope in her eyes, the way she was pleading with him to listen and not reject her. More than anything, he wanted to give her that. But he also owed it to both of them to be in a place where he could listen. Really listen. And in order to do that, there was something he needed to do.

He closed his eyes and shook his head. "No."

"No?"

"No, Ella. I can't right now." He placed his hands on her hips and as gently as he could, he lifted her off his lap and stood. "I need some time. It's been a long few days and I need a little time to think about everything that's happened. I need some time by myself to clear my head before we talk. I'm not saying no forever." He reached out to her, needing a connection, however small. "I'm not saying that at all."

Her lip quivered but she wouldn't cry. Not in front of him. He could see the strength that ran through her. "I wish it didn't feel that way." She slipped her hand out of his and stood. "I can see that you need time, Kade. I know you've been through a lot the last few days and you've learned a lot, but I'm not your family. I'm not your mom or your sister. I'm sure they had their own reasons for doing what they did, but they aren't mine."

"Ella, I know. I—"

"No, *mi amour*." She held up her finger to silence him. "You don't know. But you will. I will tell you what you need to know, when you're ready." She crossed her arms and hugged herself before she turned away.

He could see her heart breaking right in front of him. He shoved his hands in his back pockets to keep from reaching out for her again and telling her how wrong he was and how none of it mattered. He wanted to tell her all of that. But he also needed to clear his head.

He stood and watched while she walked through the kitchen door, and away from him.

The room felt small. And lonely. Chloe and Harper had done their best to make it cozy when she'd first arrived at the Ridge. Not that she'd spent any time in her little room off the kitchen. Not even one night. Until now.

She sat on the little mattress and for the first time since Gabriella had walked away from Kade that morning, she allowed herself to think about everything that had happened.

Really think about it. She'd managed to keep busy in the kitchen, making a batch of soup and prepping for dinner the next night, and other tasks that took up just enough mental energy that she didn't have to think about how Kade had sent her away. And that's exactly what he'd done. He didn't want to listen to her explanation. He didn't want to hear anything. He'd shut down.

And maybe she could understand that to some extent. Maybe she could understand that he was trying to process everything he'd learned from his grandfather, as well as her story. The timing sucked. *Dios mio. Did the timing ever suck.*

She ran her hands through her hair and lay back on the mattress.

She'd half expected him to go off and do whatever he needed to do and then come back to her. Come back and tell her that he was ready to hear her story now and he was sorry he hadn't been ready before.

But he hadn't done that.

Gabriella hadn't seen him all day and she felt his absence in her heart.

Silent tears slipped down her cheeks to the pillow. She couldn't pretend it didn't hurt. It did. And she'd never felt quite so alone as she did at the moment in the Den, in the middle of the Montana mountains in a place that for a blink of an eye, she thought she could make a life. A future.

But now...

Siempre recuerde, usted es fuerte. Cree en ti mismo y siempre encontrará el camino.

Always remember, you are strong. Believe in yourself and you will always find the way.

Her *abuela*'s voice came to her. She'd died when Gabriella was only a child, and there was no way she could've known how Gabriella's life would play out. That Carlos would be abusive, that she'd have to leave it all behind and run. But somehow, she'd always said the right things.

"I am strong."

She stared at the ceiling above her.

And with Kade, she'd have her mate. But even if he chose not to come back and listen to her, she would be okay. She'd have to be. There weren't any other options.

Gabriella swiped at her wet eyes and sat up on the bed. There was no point feeling sorry for herself. She'd been strong enough to leave her home and flee to a strange place to start over; she was definitely strong enough to handle this. Just the way her *abuela* knew she would be. She wouldn't let her grandmother down.

"Gabriella?"

A familiar voice called out. She froze. Her heart both stopped and increased its rhythm at the same time.

No. There was no way.

"*Hola*, Gabriella." The singsong tone made her stomach turn. "I know you're here."

Carlos. He was getting closer.

How did he know where she was?

It didn't matter.

He was there. In the Den. And she was alone.

Panic flashed through her. Her heart raced as she looked around the bare little room. There weren't any windows, no weapons—nothing. She couldn't stay there but the thought of opening the door and confronting him made her want to throw up.

There was no choice.

She moved quickly, opening the door and slipping out to the kitchen where at least there was an escape route. Or something to use as a weapon. Not that she planned to stick around. Coming face to face with Carlos wasn't a good idea. She needed to get out before he found her. She glanced out the window. The snow had started to come down; the wind had picked up and swirled around the yard. It made her cold just to look outside. It was going to be a big storm, but staying inside was not going to be an option for much longer.

Gabriella could hear Carlos's footsteps upstairs. He was going through the guest rooms, looking for her. He wouldn't find anyone. There was no one there. Chloe and Luke wouldn't be back until late and Harper and Axel were definitely not around. Of course, Kade might be in his cabin. He was probably in his cabin, but...it didn't matter. She needed to get out and fast.

Her parka was in the main room, along with her boots, but there was no time to get them. She'd have to slip out the back in her flats and no jacket. It wasn't ideal. It didn't matter. She grabbed a paring knife out of the knife block and tucked it into her pocket. It was better than nothing. She had her hand on the handle, ready to brace herself against the snow when she heard a voice that caused her blood to run colder than the frigid February air outside.

"*Amante.*"

Lover. It was the nickname he had for her. It made her stomach turn over every time she heard it.

She shook her head but refused to turn around. She just needed to keep moving. Open the door and run.

"You're a tricky one to track down, *amante.*"

"Don't call me that." She swallowed hard to keep her voice from shaking. Gabriella refused to let him affect her. "I am not your lover."

"Ah..." He smiled and took a step toward her. "Don't play hard to get." He stepped even closer and she sidestepped out of the way, but it took her farther from the door. From her escape. "You know I'll get you."

A chill ran up Gabriella's spine, her feet frozen to the spot.

He wouldn't get her. He wouldn't. Not this time. With a burst of energy, Gabriella lunged forward and ducked behind the counter. *He wouldn't get her. He wouldn't.*

Carlos's laugh echoed through the space, against the stainless-steel appliances and into her heart. "No, *amante*. Do not run. I don't want to hurt you."

"Yes you do." She clamped a hand over her mouth. She knew better than to fuel him. That's all it did; any outburst from her only fueled him. But she couldn't help it. He *did* want to hurt her. That's why he was here.

Wasn't it? She wasn't stupid. She'd dealt with him enough to know that.

"Ahhh, *amante*. I love you. I don't want to hurt you. I love you."

"You don't love me."

Dammit. She bit her lip, hard. She needed to stop talking. It would be best if she just shut up and spent her time figuring out how to get out of there.

"Oh, but I do." She could hear his footsteps move closer. She was definitely at a disadvantage, not being able to see him. A huge one. But she could hear him. She needed to keep him talking.

"How do you love me? How can you tell me that?"

He laughed again. The sound made her stomach turn. "If I didn't love you, would I travel all this way to find you, *amante*? Would a man who did not care do that?"

Gabriella knew exactly what he wanted to hear. "No, Carlos." It made her nauseous to say it, but she had to play his game. "Of course you love me. It's a long journey. It was good of you to come."

"Is it?"

He was playing with her. It was a game she could play.

She'd been able to talk herself out of more than one situation. Only this time, she couldn't afford to lose.

"Of course it is. How was the trip? Did it take you long?"

"Long?" He slammed his hand on the counter. "Did it take *long*?"

It was the wrong question.

"Yes, it took *long*. I didn't know where the fuck you were, Gabriella. Did you know it takes infinitely longer to find a person when you don't know where the fuck they are?" He came around the corner and delivered the last part of the sentence as he stood over her.

Menacing didn't begin to describe him. She'd been afraid of the man for way too long. But not anymore. She refused to cower under his glare again.

She pushed herself up, using the counter to brace herself until she stood in front of him. It was the closest she'd been in months. The last time had resulted in bruises that had taken weeks to fade. Her fingers twitched at her side. This time she had a knife. If he touched her again, she'd kill him.

"But I did it, *amante*." The sneer returned to his face. *How could she have ever thought he was handsome?* Where Kade was strong and rugged, Carlos was slick and small. He was taller than her, but not a large man by any standards, definitely not compared to the Jackson brothers she'd been surrounded by for the last few months.

"I looked high and low, and I found you." He kept talking as he reached out to touch her cheek. She shuddered, but didn't pull away the way every nerve in her body begged her to. She wasn't stupid. She wouldn't anger him. Not if she could help it. "Now it's time for your little holiday to end, Gabriella. It's time to come home."

She ignored him. "How did you find me?"

"Instinct, Gabriella. We're destined to be mates. You're in

my heart." He took her hand and held it to his chest. "And I am in yours." She skirted to the side before he could put his hand to her chest in turn.

It wasn't instinct. They were not destined to be mates. Kade was her mate.

Kade.

Surely he'd sense her distress. He'd come for her.

But he'd rejected her and left. He was so confused, so clouded, would his instincts even be sharp enough to sense her? There was no way of knowing.

She shook her head. "No."

"Yes, Gabriella." He squeezed her hand to the point she couldn't feel the tips of her fingers. "We are destined and we will be mated. Soon."

"No." She tried to pull her hand free. "You're hurting my hand, Carlos."

Instantly, he relaxed his grip, but didn't let go. "It's never been my intention to hurt you, Gabriella. You must know that?"

It was a line she'd heard before. It meant nothing. But it was something else he'd said that stuck with her. They would not be mated. And definitely not soon. If they mated, that would be it. She'd be locked to him. She'd have to return to Argentina. Her life would be over. She couldn't let that happen. No matter what.

"We'll leave at once," Carlos said. "I've alerted your father that I've found you and he's preparing for a small, but prompt ceremony when we arrive. Finally, *amante*, we will be mated."

Her mind spun. "But you wanted a large ceremony," she said. "The plans. The food, the guests. Everything. What about—"

"No." He pressed a finger to her lips. "We will be mated without festivity. You had your chance. Now it's just a formality. Making it official so this type of thing never happens again."

His finger turned and he grabbed her cheek in a painful grip, pulling her lips forward as he spoke.

"If it's just about the ritual, why wait?" A voice, both strangely familiar and at the same time completely new to her, spoke from somewhere behind Carlos. "From what I understand of your culture," the voice continued, "all you need is the witness of an alpha from another clan to act as witness. I'll be that witness."

Gabriella strained her neck, both to get away from Carlos's grip and also to see the mystery man, who was clearly no friend of hers.

"Good idea, Gordon."

Gordon? Kade's grandfather? No.

But she didn't have time to react and she definitely didn't have time to think. She only had time to act. And that's exactly what she did. As soon as Carlos turned his back to her, Gabriella reached into her pocket, pulled out the knife and stabbed. The force of the impact sent a shock vibrating through her arm, but she didn't have time to see where she hit him.

She turned and as fast as she could, ran out the door and out into the snow.

The wind was picking up and the sky grew darker by the minute. Although Kade should have been worried about heading back to the Den before it got worse, he just kept trudging along what he knew to be the path. Pushing himself farther in the knee-deep snow, he tucked his head down and kept moving. Luke had radioed him twenty minutes ago, right as he'd set out, to tell him they were all safe. With the building storm, he and Chloe had made the call to stop at the nearest shelter, which was Blackwood Ranch, about ten miles down the road from Grizzly Ridge. They were tucked in with the Blackwoods, a group of wolves who'd proved to be more ally than enemy over the months, and they'd be safe until morning.

Which meant Ella was on her own at the Den.

He should go back.

But he couldn't.

Not until he did what he'd come out there to do.

What he *needed* to do. He needed to shift.

But he couldn't.

It should be easy. It was natural. He'd been doing it all his life, shifting into his bear and running through the woods. It had never been difficult before. He'd never *not* been able to shift. Hell, he'd pushed his bear down for months; he should be more than ready to let his animal out.

He was blocked. But he wasn't going back until he sorted it out. Ella had a story to tell, but he wasn't going to be any good to her until he dealt with the wild animal inside him.

Kade.

"Ella?" He turned in the snow, searching the path around him, certain he'd heard her. *Was she calling him? Was she in trouble?* He squeezed his eyes shut, trying in vain to connect with her, but there was nothing. He couldn't even sense her. He was so wildly disconnected from his bear that his instincts were off. And the connection he did have with Ella had only blurred things even more instead of fine-tuning it the way it should have done.

Kade dug the radio out of his pocket and held the button down, speaking loudly because of the wind. "Luke. Come in, Luke."

It took a moment, but the radio crackled to life. "Kade? I'm here. Everything okay?"

"Ella." It was the only word he could manage. Just saying her name conjured an image of distress. *Something was wrong.*

"Ella? What about her?"

Kade swallowed hard and pressed through. "I need you to check on her."

"You're not with her?"

"No."

There was a moment of silence. "Where are you, Kade?"

He tried in vain again to pick up on Ella. "I need you to check on her," he repeated. "Something's wrong."

"What's going on, Kade?"

He shook his head. "I don't know. But something isn't right."

"Where are you?"

"I'm headed to the ridge."

He pulled the collar of his jacket up higher around his face and kept walking. He needed to get to the ridge to set his bear free.

Kade.

Once again, he stopped in his tracks. The hair on the back of his neck bristled.

That *was* Ella.

Despite everything that had happened and continued to happen, he *knew* his mate. Ella needed him. He spun helplessly in the growing white-out. *But where was she? Who was she with? What was wrong?*

He once again pulled the radio to his mouth. "Luke, something's wrong. Really wrong. I'm going to find her."

The tension in his body grew. His heart raced. The heat of his own body was too much and he shucked his parka into the snowbank, followed by his shirt. He stood half naked in the blizzard, but his skin was on fire, his animal growing more and more agitated.

He stuck his nose into the air, but still he couldn't get a read on her. He needed his bear. *Now.*

He shut his eyes, focused on the feeling of transforming,

tried to channel every bit of his energy into his animal and...nothing.

"Dammit."

It wasn't working. But it could work. It had to. He was a grizzly, for God's sake. He'd *make* it happen.

Ella.

That was it.

It was Ella. She was the key and despite everything, it didn't matter. He wanted to be with her and his bear *needed* to be with her. And if anything happened to her, he wouldn't be able to live with himself and *that* was why he was going to do exactly what he needed to do to protect his mate.

A roar ripped from his throat. The sound thundered through the forest despite the muffling snow. His core temperature rose to an almost intolerable level until finally, he felt the always familiar stretch and pull of his muscles as they shifted around him. He dropped the radio into the snow and lunged himself forward, throwing his body up and into the air at the exact moment his bear took over.

CHAPTER THIRTEEN

THE SNOW BIT into her feet, numbing her toes in only the first few steps, but she kept moving. She had to. As quickly as she could. Gabriella couldn't even feel her feet by the time she found the snow-covered path that led to the cabins. But it didn't matter. If it hadn't been for the adrenaline flowing through her body, she might have felt the biting cold stinging her face, her bare arms, and every inch of exposed skin. But she didn't. The only thing she could think of was....*run*. She needed to get as far away from Carlos and Gordon as possible. Hopefully the knife bought her enough time to get help.

But there was no help. Reflexively, she'd been running to Kade's cabin. She'd been running to Kade. Despite whatever was going on between them, he'd help her. She knew it. She felt it.

But something was wrong. She couldn't sense him nearby. It didn't mean he wasn't there, but...

Behind her, down by the Den, she heard a door slam. They were coming after her. And she had no doubt exactly what would happen when they caught her.

No. If they caught her.

And they wouldn't. Her future, her safety...her life depended on getting away.

With one last glance toward Kade's cabin, she veered to the right and the next instant, the familiar stretching of her muscles took over. She heard the tearing of her clothing as she shifted into her bear.

"What the—"

Gabriella couldn't help but feel a small sense of satisfaction at Carlos's reaction behind her. He'd never seen her shift into her bear before. As far as he was concerned, she hadn't shifted since she was a girl, and then only in supervised situations. But she was definitely no stranger to her bear anymore, and that was absolutely working to her advantage as she headed into the woods, running as fast as she could in the deep snow.

Visibility decreased as the wind picked up. There was a bit more shelter in the trees, but with the thick cover on the ground, it was hard to see the obstacles that kept slowing her down. Gabriella stumbled on fallen logs, branches, and other debris hidden by the snow, but she had to believe the men would be slowed down by the same things. She wasn't totally sure where she was going, and had very little plan in place except to put as much distance between her and Carlos as possible. She definitely had an advantage from her almost nightly runs in the woods with the others. She was no longer a complete stranger to the trees and trails, and Carlos certainly wouldn't know his way around.

Gordon might.

Grizzly Ridge, after all, had been part of his land once before he banished his grandsons to it. Gabriella had no idea whether that meant he'd spent any time there or not, but she couldn't let herself think about it. Instinct told her to run to the Ridge and that's exactly where she was headed. Once she got there, she'd be able to follow the line down into town. If she moved quickly, she'd hopefully be able to find somewhere warm to spend the night before she needed to shift back. Once she shifted back into her human form, she'd freeze even faster. She had to move quickly.

A roar behind her caused her stomach to tense. *Carlos.* The knife hadn't slowed him down too much. He was in pursuit and he was pissed. She'd recognize that sound anywhere. It had once been accompanied with a punch or slap. But no more. Now, she'd only use the sound to fuel her.

Never again.

She wasn't going back.

Gabriella channeled all her memories, fear, and anger into moving as fast as she could. She had a bit of a head start, but Gordon was a bigger, stronger bear. If he hadn't had age working against him, there was no doubt he would have caught her right away. As it was, she was able to stay slightly ahead of him. But only slightly. When she broke through the tree line on the ridge, she didn't feel the sense of relief she'd been counting on. Ahead of her, instead of the deep blue sky or star-filled night sky she was used to seeing on the ridge, all she saw was gray.

Up so high in a storm, the wind whipped the snow all around until finally Gabriella wasn't even sure what direction she was facing. She turned but could no longer see the trees.

Where's the ridge? She stopped and turned. *Where are they?* She couldn't see them, but she knew they were close. They had to be.

In answer to her unasked question, there was a growl behind her. In reflex, she took a step forward, and realized at once exactly where the ridge was.

Right in front of her. She was close to the edge. Dangerously close.

But the danger behind her was more than real. She could feel the beast was close. Way too close.

There was no other choice. She swallowed hard, swung her head around and roared as loud as she could before she lunged toward Gordon. It was practically a suicide mission given that the old grizzly was so much bigger than her. But he was old, and Gabriella was quick. And pissed off. She bared her teeth and dug into the bear's flank, biting down as hard as she could. Gordon squealed, a terrible noise that turned into a menacing growl, but Gabriella only had seconds to register it before a solid blow hit her on the side of the head. She flew through the air and landed hard in the snow.

She was cold. So cold. And her head hurt. Darkness crept around the edges of her vision and she fought hard to stay conscious. If she closed her eyes...she couldn't....she couldn't let that happen. A shadow fell over her. Carlos. Snarling. His teeth bared.

He couldn't. He wouldn't.

Gabriella tried to lift her head but it was too heavy and pain shot across her temple.

Carlos snarled again, and took another step so he was almost on top of her. In her peripheral vision, a grizzly appeared.

All you need is a clan alpha as witness.

She growled, but even to her own ears, it sounded more like a whimper and she hated herself for it. She hated that it would end like this. After all her strength, he would take what he wanted and there wasn't a damn thing she'd be able to do about it. A tear slipped from her eye and froze in her fur.

She blinked hard in an effort to clear her vision, but it was no use. The last thing Gabriella heard as she slipped into unconsciousness was the loud, angry roar of the one meant to be her mate.

Kade.

It only took him a moment to remember exactly what it felt like to experience his bear. One moment of uncertainty. One moment of hesitation. And then it was gone and Kade was running. His muscles protested initially at the stretching and pulling, but soon enough his body warmed up and any hesitation he'd felt was gone as he pushed himself through the woods in the direction of the ridge.

He pushed himself to his limit. If it had been under any other circumstance, he would have warmed up into the shift. He would have taken some time to walk around and get comfortable with his animal again. But he was definitely not under any normal circumstances. Nothing was normal. Everything was wrong.

Ella.

Ella.

He focused on his mate. It didn't take long until his body was adjusted to his animal again and his heightened senses homed in on her. She was at the Ridge. She wasn't alone. And she was in trouble.

Kade ran harder, faster. His breath came in pants. His body screamed in protest to the exertion, but it didn't matter. He wouldn't slow down for anything. Not until he knew his mate was safe.

Why would she be out in a storm?

She was from Peru, for God's sake.

Argentina, he corrected himself.

It didn't matter. It didn't. Wherever she was from, whatever her name really was. None of that really mattered because the only thing that mattered in that moment was making sure she was okay. She'd lied. That much *was* true. But she would have a reason for lying to him. A reason he hadn't wanted to hear because he selfishly thought he needed to take care of himself first. And it was selfish, because if he was going to have a mate—

and he *was* going to have a mate—she had to come first. No matter what. And that's exactly what he was going to do. He was going to put her first. There'd be time to hear everything she had to say, and it wouldn't matter either.

Whatever her reasons were for running from her clan and lying to him...they didn't matter. The only thing that mattered was that they would be together.

The snow was coming harder and the wind had picked up since he'd started out on his hike. The cold bit through his fur, but he hardly felt it.

Ella would feel it.

Even with her fur coat, she wasn't made for a Montana winter. A bespectacled bear had no business running around in a blizzard.

Assuming she was in her bear form.

He couldn't tell. He was so out of touch with his instincts, and his senses, although now firing, were still out of practice. He couldn't be sure. He could only be sure that it was her he ran toward.

A roar echoed through the trees, pulling him out of his thoughts and stopping him mid-stride.

Ella?

No.

A second later, another roar.

That *was* Ella.

They were close. And she was in trouble.

Kade pounded through the deepening snow and broke through the tree line just in time to see one of the biggest grizzlies he'd ever seen reach out and swipe at his mate with his paw. She went flying like a rag doll, landing in the snow with a thud. Kade growled low in his throat, but neither the grizzly nor the other, smaller bear seemed to have heard him. He took a minute to catch his breath and assess the situation. The smaller bear looked to be a bespectacled bear as well. *Maybe someone she knew from back home?* But the grizzly...

He didn't have time to think about it too hard as the smaller bear stalked over to his mate. Even from a distance, Kade could see he'd bared his teeth.

His heart beat so hard and fast, Kade couldn't even see straight. His gaze locked on Ella lying helplessly in the snowbank as the other bear approached.

There was no way in hell he'd let anyone hurt his mate.

With a roar that was probably heard all through the ridge, Kade crossed the space and lunged through the air, connecting hard with the smaller bear.

Whoever he was, he was so much smaller that he wasn't much of a match for Kade. Kade easily dominated him, pinning him beneath him with his paws. The other bear growled and bared his teeth. If it was any other opponent, Kade would have let him up, let him go. But this bear tried to hurt his mate. He swiped at him, leaving a trail of claw marks that welled up red against the snow. Kade growled one more time to make his point. If he thought the cuts were bad, he'd happily make sure his point was taken. Subdued for the moment, Kade swung his heavy head around to find the next threat.

The grizzly.

But the grizzly wasn't a threat. He stood silently. Watching.

And Kade could see why.

His dark fur was shaggy and dulled with age. It was hard to tell with the snow whipping around, but Kade was pretty sure if he could look closer, he'd see the gray fur flecked throughout. Of that he had no doubt. It had been a long time since he'd seen his grandfather in his bear. But there was no question that it was Gordon who stood and watched.

The only question was...why. Why was his grandfather

attacking his mate? Surely he couldn't be so filled with hate that he'd want to hurt someone he didn't even know.

But he'd have to wait to ask his questions. Kade's ears pricked to attention at the sound of a snowmobile approaching from the distance. *Luke.* He'd be there soon.

The large grizzly heard the noise, too. He shook his head slowly, turned and headed back into the trees.

A second later, Kade was hit from behind. The bespectacled bear had found his second wind. Either that or he had a death wish. Being so much bigger than the other bear, Kade barely moved from the impact. He turned quickly and with his massive paw, swiped at the smaller bear, leaving another trail of bloody tracks on his fur. For good measure, Kade swiped again, and lunged toward the bear. Kade held his throat between his heavy jaws. All he had to do was close and he'd end it.

And there was a large part of him that wanted nothing more than to do just that. This bear dared to attack Ella. He didn't deserve to live.

The sound of Ella whimpering behind him jarred him from his task. With a growl, he shoved the bear away. And just to keep him from getting up until Kade was ready for him to do so, he landed one more blow against the bear's head before he turned his attention to his mate.

Ella whimpered again and a second later, shifted back to her human form.

She still wasn't conscious, and without shelter, she'd freeze to death.

Kade was shaky and running off what little adrenaline he had left, but he wasn't sure he could stay in his bear much longer. It had been so long since he'd shifted, and his run through the woods had taken so much out of him. But as long as Ella was in danger, there was no way he'd succumb to the exhaustion. As gently as he could, he moved himself around her, and used his paws to lift her so she was resting on his fur, before he folded his body over top of her to shelter her from the blowing snow.

She was so cold.

Come on, Ella. Hang in there.

I love you.

CHAPTER FOURTEEN

SHE WAS COLD.

So cold.

And her head. It throbbed unbearably.

With her eyes still closed, she moved a hand up to touch her forehead.

A hand. Bare skin.

She wasn't in her bear anymore. She should be freezing to death. *Was she...did Carlos...*

Her eyes snapped open and she tried to sit up, but was met with instant pain and laid back on the pillow. She was in a bed. There were blankets.

She squeezed her eyes shut and tried to move through each part of her body with her mind, searching for extra pains, bite marks—anything. Any evidence that Carlos had mated with her while she'd been unconscious.

"Ella."

She opened her eyes once more at the sound of Kade's voice. Tears sprang to her eyes and ran unchecked down her cheeks at the sight of him. She tried to lift her head again.

"No," he said. In a moment, he was at her side. "Lay down.

You took quite a blow to the head." His touch on her forehead was gentle and warm on her skin. "How are you feeling?"

"I'm...did...what..." She couldn't formulate a thought. Not a coherent one, anyway. She wanted to ask him whether Carlos had mated her, whether she was compromised in any way. But she couldn't find the words to ask what she needed to. Not with Kade. If it was true...if he had...she couldn't stand the thought and what it would mean.

"Hey." Kade's fingers gently wiped her tears, but they kept coming. Now that she'd started, she couldn't seem to stop. "It's okay," he said. "You're safe now."

"Am I?" She choked back a sob. "Am I really?"

Kade sat on the bed, the mattress sinking with his weight, and pulled her into his arms. "Yes." He looked in her eyes. "You're safe now. We got your attacker and Luke has him in the shed for now until we can figure out what's going on."

"Kade, I can—"

"Shh. Not now, babe. Rest. And when you're ready, I know you'll fill in all the blanks. But first you need to rest."

"No. I need to tell you."

"Whatever you need to tell me can wait." He smiled and kissed her forehead. His gentleness was in such a contrast to his overwhelming size, but never had Gabriella felt safer and more loved than in that moment. And she believed him; whatever she needed to tell him, it could wait and she knew in her heart that he wouldn't walk away from her again. Whatever restlessness there had been in him earlier was gone.

"Okay," she finally agreed. "But we need to talk later."

He kissed her forehead again. "Absolutely. Because I want to know everything about my mate."

Mate. The word sent a shiver of pleasure through her because for the first time, she knew he meant it and everything that would come with it. She could *feel* it.

"Are you done with her?" The door opened and Chloe came in, carrying a tray. "I want my turn," she said. "Before I have to go down to town." She set the tray on the table next to the bed and leaned down to give Gabriella a gentle hug. "Are you okay? That was all...it was just crazy."

"It was," she agreed. "I'm glad you're here, Chloe. I need to tell you something. I just wish Harper was here, too."

"She can be." Kade went out into the main room and returned a few moments later with an iPad. "Let's pull her up on FaceTime." It only took a few clicks of a button and Harper's face filled the screen.

"Oh my goodness, Ella! I can't believe I'm not there. Are you okay? I heard what happened. Well...most of it. Are you okay?"

Gabriella smiled. "I am. Well, I will be now. How are you doing?"

"Don't worry about me." Harper waved her concern away. "This little guy is just letting me know that he'll be exactly like his father one day." She laughed and it spread to the small group crowded around Gabriella's bed as well.

A second later, the view widened and Axel appeared next to his mate. The sight of him sparked something in Gabriella.

A trail of fear crept down her spine and she hadn't realized she'd started shaking until Kade grabbed her hands in his. "Gabriella, what's wrong?"

"It's...Axel...no." She shook her head. "Not Axel. But...your grandfather." She looked up at Kade. The expression told her that he already knew. "I forgot until right now," she continued. "But he was there. It had to have been him. He has the same coloring as Axel. The same eyes."

"It was him," Kade confirmed.

"Is he...was he..." She wasn't sure how to finish the question.

"After I got there, he wasn't a threat. He left and I let him go because you were my primary concern. I needed to keep you warm until help arrived."

"And Luke got there as soon as he could," Chloe added.

Gabriella's mind spun. There was so much she didn't know about what had happened after she lost consciousness. She didn't know where to begin or how to put the pieces together.

Kade must have seen the confusion in her eyes. "I was walking in the woods." He spoke only to her. "I needed to...I needed to figure things out with myself." He didn't need to explain that part; Gabriella understood completely. "And then I felt you," he continued. "I felt you were in trouble. I had just enough time to radio Luke before I shifted and went after you."

"Wait." The impact of what he'd just said reverberated through her. *He'd shifted. He'd connected with his bear.* "You—"

He cut her off with a slight nod. "Getting to you as quickly as I could was just what I needed. It was instinct."

"To protect your mate," Chloe said softly.

"I got there just in time." He closed his eyes, as if it was painful to recount, which it very likely was, but Gabriella needed to hear it. She needed to know. "I took care of him, your attacker, but it wasn't my grandfather. He was just...standing there. And then he left."

"I'm going to take care of him," Axel said from the screen. "Just as soon as you get here, Chloe. I'm going to find him and I'll get answers."

She believed him. The Jackson brothers cared about her. They all did.

"He was with Carlos," she said. "Why would he be with Carlos?"

"Carlos?"

Gabriella nodded at Chloe's question. "My ex." Her eyes never left Kade's. "That's what I was trying to tell you. I'm sorry. Given the circumstances, it can't wait."

"Okay. If you're feeling up to it, I'm ready to listen to whatever you need to tell me. And Ella?" She blinked hard, determined to hold back tears until she had finished saying what needed to be said. "Whatever you say, it won't change how I feel about you. It won't change how much I love you, now and forever. You need to know that."

"Even though I lied?" She bit down hard on her lip and looked to Chloe and the others on the screen. "I lied to you all. I'm sorry. But I was running. For my life."

Everyone was silent while she spoke, filling them in on Carlos and the abuse she'd experienced at his hand and would no doubt continue to if she hadn't run. "It's not like here," she said when she had finished telling them the details. "I know every clan has their situations, but..."

"They're not abusive." Chloe grabbed her hand and squeezed. "Ella, what you went through...to run away like that..." Tears streaked down the other woman's cheeks. "You're so incredibly strong."

"You are, Ella." Harper blew her nose loudly. "I wish I was there to give you a hug right now."

"*Gracias, mi amigas.*" The words seemed so ineffective. "Thank you." But there was nothing else to say. Kade hadn't said anything since she'd finished her story, ending with how she'd arrived at the Ridge. He sat silently at her side, her other hand in his; his thumb stroked small circles on the surface. "Kade?"

"I should have killed him when I had the chance." The words were barely a whisper, but Gabriella heard them crystal-clear and she knew right away it wasn't the answer. "I had him right there," Kade continued. "Right beneath me, the weak coward. I should have—"

"No." Gabriella put her hand on his arm. "No, Kade. He can't—" She stopped because there was still one thing she needed to be sure of. "He didn't...I mean, you got there in time, right?" She swallowed hard. The words were too hard to get out. "He didn't *mate* me..."

Kade stiffened, his whole body rigid and tense. "If he had, he *would* be dead right now."

The sense of relief that washed through her was almost enough to break her. She'd tried so hard to hold herself together, but the relief was almost too much.

"Okay." Chloe jumped up from the bed. "I think that's my cue to leave. And time to shut you two off." She held the iPad up. "I'll be right there so you can leave, Axel."

"I can stay on my own, you know," Harper protested. "You guys take care of what you need—"

Chloe's cell phone rang, interrupting the debate.

"It's Luke." She answered and was silent as she listened for a moment before she said, "Okay. I'll tell him."

When she ended the call, she looked right at Kade. "That was Luke. Your grandfather just showed up. He wants to talk to all three of you."

She'd insisted on coming, and although he would have preferred she'd stayed in bed, Kade was also happy to have her within sight. Even if it meant she was also within sight of the man who'd attacked her.

Carlos.

He still didn't know much about her ex, but all he did know was enough for him to hate the man. Only a cowardly, little man disrespected a woman by laying a hand on her. Just thinking about him touching Ella in any way was enough for Kade's bear to roar to the surface. He settled his mate in a chair next to the workbench, as far away from both Carlos and his grandfather as he could manage.

As far as Carlos was concerned, Luke had the weasel tied securely to a chair. He looked as if he'd had better days. Clearly the beating Kade had given him had made a point. If Kade could have arranged it, he would have tied up their grandfather right next to him. It didn't matter what his involvement was in what had happened to Ella; the only thing that mattered was that he *was* involved. They'd agreed to wait for Axel to arrive, before hearing what he had to say, but being in the same room with him was too much. His bear was close to the surface. Too close. Now that he'd rediscovered his bear, he had a very hard time controlling it. Especially where Ella was concerned.

He stalked across the room until he was only inches from his grandfather. He looked even older and more frail than the last time he'd seen him.

"Talk."

"We should wait for Axel."

"He can catch up." Kade didn't bother to look over at Luke. "I want answers now."

There was no way Luke would argue with him, and Kade knew it. If it had been Chloe who'd been attacked and almost... no. He couldn't think about what could have happened out there on the ridge. But if it had been Chloe, or Harper who'd been in that position, Kade wouldn't begrudge them finding out what happened. And they both knew it.

He turned his attention back to his grandfather. "What are you doing here? What do you have to do with this?"

"I told Carlos where to find Gabriella."

Whatever answer Kade was expecting from his grandfather, it wasn't that. A growl from deep inside him rose up, and he could feel his teeth sharpen in his mouth.

"Her father contacted me, just as he had all the clan alphas, at least a month earlier." He moved his head to the side he could see around Kade to Ella. "They've been looking a long time for you, young lady. You're very important to—"

"Don't talk to her," Kade growled. "Don't you ever talk to her again."

"Kade," Ella said. "It's okay. I'm okay."

He shook his head, but didn't take his eyes off his grandfather. "How did you know where she was?"

"You told me."

The air rushed from his lungs. "What? No. I would never—"

"When you came to visit, Kade. I asked you about your mate."

"She's *my* mate."

Kade didn't look, but he heard a thud followed by a groan, which more than likely was the sound of his brother taking care of Carlos's outburst.

"You asked me who she was," Kade said, trying desperately to remember the conversation. "I told you she was from Peru. And now I know..." He looked at Ella, who smiled encouragingly. "But, I didn't—"

"It was enough to go on," Gordon said. "There aren't a lot of South American bear shifters in the Montana mountains. I knew right away who she was."

The rage filled Kade again. "So you sold her out. How much did they give you for that information?"

"Nothing." Gordon leaned against the shed wall. Despite his anger, Kade could see how exhausted the old man looked. "It's code, Kade. It's just the—"

"Do not tell me it's just the way things are done. I suppose helping this asshole attack my mate is also part of the code, is it?"

"Kade...it's not." His grandfather shrugged in defeat. "Fine.

Yes. There's no point in lying to you boys any more than I already have. I came here with Carlos to help him claim Gabriella so he could take her back to his clan. In fact, I suggested he do it now and not wait."

"You son of a—"

Luke put a hand on his shoulder and held him back, which was probably the only thing that kept him from killing his grandfather right there on the spot.

"You were going to *help* him? But once she was..." Kade shook his head in an effort to clear the murderous thoughts forming there. It didn't work. "I should kill you now." He glared at Carlos, too. "Both of you."

"Kade." Her voice was weak—she'd been through so much— but it penetrated to the heart of him. "*Por favor, mi amour.*"

He went to her side. "Are you okay?"

"I'm fine." She smiled, and his heart clenched in his chest.

He'd come so close to losing her. And why? Because he'd needed to find himself? When everything he'd ever needed to know about himself was right there in front of him. In Ella. He'd been so stupid. It would never be worth it to leave her like that again. And if she let him, he'd spend the rest of his life making sure she was safe.

"I'm healing quickly, Kade. But I don't think my heart could ever heal if you killed your grandfather because of me."

"But he's—"

"Your grandfather. *Su familia.* No matter what's happened, that will never change."

He shook his head and couldn't look her in the eyes. Not when he didn't care whether Gordon was family or not. He didn't care whether he was the only family they had left: he'd tried to hurt his mate. Kade would never forgive him for that and he knew Luke and Axel wouldn't stop him if he tried.

The door opened and Axel walked in with a rush of snow.

"What's going on?" His eyes landed on Gordon and then traveled across the room to where Kade stood by Ella. "I'm surprised they're not dead by now," he said. "Kade's not known for his reason these days."

"You have every right to kill me, Kade." Gordon's voice was tired, but still strong. "And if that's what you want, I won't blame you. I don't think your brothers would either. But I would like a chance to say something first."

He squeezed Ella's hand in assurance. He wouldn't hurt anyone if it was going to upset her. He would never do anything to upset her. Not again. Not even if his entire being wanted to make his grandfather pay for the role he'd played. For Ella, he wouldn't.

He once again crossed the room until he loomed over his grandfather, who seemed smaller and more frail as the minutes ticked by. "Go ahead," he said. "Talk."

Gordon swallowed hard. Never before had Kade seen the man as anything other than formidable. Things had changed. "The other day when you came to visit me, Kade, I realized something. I realized how much I missed my boys. I realized how lonely my life was. When you left, you left a hole."

"We didn't leave," Axel said. "You kicked us out."

"I know. And I did what I thought I had to do at the time." Gordon looked around the room at all of them. "You have to understand. I've only ever done what I thought was best. I did what I thought I had to in order to protect our clan. Our kind. But in trying to protect us, I destroyed us."

He sounded genuine. Kade wanted to believe that he was genuine. But there was one thing that didn't make sense. "If this is true, then why did you help Carlos? Why would you try to destroy the happiness I was only starting to find? If you really mean any of what you said, then explain that."

"Of course." Gordon shifted on his feet, but he stared Kade directly in the eye. "Because I didn't believe."

"Didn't believe what?"

"I didn't believe in fated mates, Kade. Even after everything with your mother. I still didn't believe."

"And Kira."

Gordon ignored that, and continued. "I didn't believe in it until I saw you come out of the trees and attack Carlos. You sensed her."

"Of course I sensed her."

"And it wasn't just that. It was the way you protected her. I could feel the connection between the two of you. I've never, in all my years, experienced that. There's no doubt in my mind that you and Gabriella are fated mates and that's why I'm here. I came to apologize. To all of you."

"Now?" Luke spoke up. "Why now? Why not when Axel and I met our mates? What makes you think we'll accept your apology now?"

Gordon took a step away from the wall, but Kade growled, keeping him in place. "I don't know if you will," he said. "And I don't blame you if you don't. But I had to try. Because now I've seen it. Now I believe. And Luke? I'm sure I'll believe just as much when I see you with your mate. And you, Axel, with yours. But I can't speak to that right now. I can't change the past," he continued. "But as a sign of good faith, I'd like to offer to take Carlos back to Argentina, to return him to his clan. I will personally guarantee he leaves and Gabriella will be safe."

"Damn straight she'll be safe," Kade growled. "I'm here."

"Of course. I just meant, I'd—"

"It's a good offer, Kade." Axel, always the voice of reason, put a hand on his arm. "It won't fix everything, but it's a start."

It was a start and it solved the immediate problem of getting

Carlos out of there before Kade changed his mind and killed him after all. He walked a few steps away, trying to find a reason that it wouldn't work. Something to object to. "Fine." He nodded after a moment. "Do it. Take him away. Just get him out of here." He turned and stared at his grandfather again. "As for you..."

"Kade." It was Axel again. "Don't say anything you'll regret."

He stared long and hard at his grandfather before he finally shook his head and looked away. "To him? I'm not going to say anything at all."

And he wasn't. His grandfather might think he could march into their lives, apologize and make it all better for everyone. And maybe he could. But not for him. The only person Kade was worried about was still sitting in the corner. But not for long.

Ignoring everyone else, Kade walked over to Ella and held out his hand. "I can't believe I've had you sitting here for so long when there's something so much more important we should be doing."

She didn't even have to ask what he was talking about, but took his hand and let him pull her up out of the chair. He wrapped his arm around her and tucked her small body into his side.

"Are you ready?" he asked her.

"For my whole life, Kade." She looked up into his eyes, and the love he saw reflected back at him told Kade everything he'd ever need to know. It was time.

No.

It was way past time.

CHAPTER FIFTEEN

THE WHOLE DAY had been more than exhausting. If Gabriella stopped to let herself think about everything they'd been through in only one short day, she would have been even more tired. And the last thing she wanted, being there in Kade's cabin, was to be exhausted.

She tried to convince him that she was more than capable of walking up the pathway to the cabin, but still he insisted on carrying her. Honestly, she liked the way he took care of her, even though both of them knew she was more than capable of caring for herself. His cabin was cold when they got there, and he settled her on the couch with a pile of blankets as he stoked the fire.

His strong back was outlined by shadows as he fed the fire and gently nursed the flames into a roaring glow. The longer Gabriella sat and watched her mate working hard to care for her, the more turned on she became. Despite everything they'd been through, he still wanted her and everything she came with. More than that, she wanted him.

She was so consumed with her thoughts that Gabriella

didn't notice he was done with the fire until he'd positioned himself right in front of her. "Are you warm enough?"

She tried to gesture with her hands, but there were so many blankets piled on top of her that she could only laugh. "I'm fine, Kade. Honestly. I'm okay."

"You've been through a lot today." As he spoke, his hands worked their way under the blankets to find her. "I just want to make sure that you have everything you need."

"I have you." Her smile radiated from her heart. And never had she spoken truer words. If she had Kade, she had everything.

"That's not all you have." His hand made its way through the layer of blankets to her thigh, where he squeezed.

"Oh yeah? What else do I have?"

Kade rose up so his face was only inches from hers. "Not only do you have me, Ella. You have everything I can offer you. The Ridge, this family: I want to give you everything. Forever." He kissed her then, and Gabriella's heart melted into a puddle at her feet as his hands cupped her cheeks, his lips moving on hers, making her body come alive.

She struggled against the weight of the blankets Kade had piled on her small body and they both ended up in giggles as she worked her way free. "I swear," she said. "If I didn't know better, I would think you were trying to trap me with all these blankets."

Instantly, she knew she'd said the wrong thing.

"I'd never trap you, Ella. I'd never do anything to hurt you. You know that, right?"

"Of course." With her arms free, she reached up and pulled him down to her. "I've never felt safer than I have when I'm with you, Kade. With you, I feel like I'm finally where I need to be. I know you'd never hurt me."

"I'd die before that happened, Ella."

He stood and pulled a soft wool blanket off the pile she'd managed to shed. While she watched, Kade spread it on the floor in front of the fire, followed by two more blankets and more pillows than she'd ever seen in the entire cabin. When he had finished, he'd created a very cozy nest for the two of them.

"It looks perfect." She stood. "But you're missing one thing."

He jumped up. "What? I'll get it. Whatever it is."

Gabriella managed to free herself from the last remaining blanket that had been wrapped around her. She dropped it on the pile and gently pushed Kade to the floor. "I can get it," she said. "I'm perfectly capable, you know?"

He licked his lips and smiled a smile so sexy it could have melted her on the spot if she'd let it. "Oh, I know, babe. You're capable of quite a lot."

She swallowed back the trace of nerves that kept sneaking up. "Then sit. I'll be right back." Gabriella could feel his eyes on her back as she walked across the cabin to the corner where she knew he kept the wine. She selected a bottle of red from the shelf, along with two glasses and a corkscrew. Aware of her audience, she was sure to stick out her behind and wiggle it just a little as she worked the cork out of the bottle and poured them each a glass before she made her way back to the rug of blankets.

"Are you going to get down here or not?"

She handed him a glass of wine and took a long, slow sip of her own. "Soon enough, *mi amour*." Gabriella knew she was teasing him, but she was also more than aware of what a special night it was going to be. She wanted to remember it, every second of it.

"In due time," she said. "But first..." She put her glass down on the coffee table and turned her attention to her clothes. She was wearing far too many of them. She remedied the situation by slipping her sweater off over her head. "I just need to be a bit more comfortable."

"By all means." The glint in his eye told her he was totally on board with whatever she wanted to do that involved removing clothes.

"And really," she continued. "These pants are just too constricting." Gabriella tugged her yoga pants down over her hips before she shimmied out of them completely. She didn't miss the way Kade's eyes widened when he saw her panties so she took the opportunity to bend over, being sure her ass was fully displayed to him before she took a drink of wine.

"Babe," he groaned. "That's a dangerous game to play."

"That's a game I'd love to play." She put the wine down, licked her lips and with a little wiggle, pulled her t-shirt over her head, leaving her only in her bra and panties.

"I see that."

Before she knew what he was doing, Kade wrapped his arms around her waist and pulled her down to the pile of blankets, and him. "And if we play correctly, it'll be a game we'll both win." He kissed her then, and she kissed him back with a passion she'd only ever felt for him.

She laid her body flat against his, feeling small in his arms, but every bit more than enough for him. She could have let him kiss her all night, but there was something she needed to do. And only she could do it.

"Take your clothes off."

Kade grinned, but didn't hesitate to comply with the order because damn, she was sexy when she was telling him what to do. "Isn't that supposed to be my line?"

"Maybe," she said. "But I don't have any clothes left, so it's your turn. Besides, I want you naked."

"Yes, ma'am."

He wiggled out to the side and quickly shed himself of his clothes before he returned to the blankets and the beautiful woman waiting for him there. But beautiful wasn't the word to describe Ella. She was amazing in every way. Her cinnamon-tinted skin shone in the firelight as the light danced off the planes of her body. Her curves only looked more delectable in the half light. His bear rose to the surface, eager to sink his teeth into her soft flesh and claim what was his, once and for all.

"Just the way I want you." Gabriella once again climbed over top of him. "I've been waiting way too long for this."

That was the biggest understatement he'd heard all night. In years, maybe. He'd waited his whole life to have a woman like her—no, a woman who *was* her. And he wasn't about to waste one more second. It was time to make his claim.

He wrapped his arms around her. In a swift move, he flipped her over so she was on her back and he hovered over top. "These are very pretty panties," he said without looking at them. "But they need to go." With a flick of his wrist, he tore the lacy material that covered her, replacing the fabric with his fingers. She was wet, and more than ready, just the way he knew she'd be. His lips found hers again and he kissed her thoroughly, as his fingers teased her. The moan that slipped from her lips told Kade all he needed to know. "I want you, Gabriella." He used her given name for the first time. "I've wanted you from the moment I laid eyes on you."

She pressed herself into him, and there was no holding back. He couldn't go slow. With one solid thrust, he was inside her. She squeezed her eyes shut, and groaned her pleasure as he sat inside for a moment, allowing her to grow used to his size. The moment she opened her eyes, he started to move inside her. Slowly at first, allowing the passion between them to build.

"Kade?" He paused and leaned down so he could hear what she needed to say. "*Tu eres mio.*" He opened his mouth to ask her what that meant, but in the next second, her teeth sank into the flesh over his shoulder blade, and he knew exactly what it meant because he felt it too.

"Gabriella, I want you, too." And not to be outdone, Kade bared his teeth and sank them into the flesh just above her collarbone. Just as she'd done to him, he finally claimed his mate.

EPILOGUE

JUNE

Walking along the ridge was still one of Gabriella's favorite things to do. Especially now that the snow had melted. It was June already, but Chloe still liked to remind her that when it came to the mountains of Montana, snow could happen at any time. She tried not to think about that. The winter had been long.

But it had also been pretty damn cozy. Gabriella stole a glance at her mate, who walked next to her.

Winters in Montana might be a whole lot different than what she was used to, but she didn't mind the cold too much as long as she had Kade to cuddle up to and keep her warm. And that had definitely helped her winter go by quickly. Very quickly.

Since they'd finally mated and she'd claimed him, followed very quickly by him claiming her, their life had been almost like a fairy tale. With all their secrets out in the open, they were free to be together without the weight of past lives weighting them down. And it had been easy and fun and just...more than she ever would have thought.

The sun was out, making the afternoon even warmer than normal, and Kade had shed his jacket. She couldn't help it; Gabriella felt a little thrill every time she saw her mate in only a t-shirt because she could see the very edge of the mark she left on him when she'd claimed him. Her hand instinctively went to her own shoulder blade. The scar almost seemed to heat up at the very memory of the night when she'd decided to take matters into her own hands.

"Are you thinking about it again?" Gabriella hadn't noticed Kade coming up beside her until she was in his arms. "I can see it in your eyes."

"I'm not," she lied, knowing he could see right through her.

He kissed her before he worked his mouth down her neck to the collar of her shirt. With a growl, he pushed it aside and revealed her mark. His claim on her. "Don't forget, babe. I have my claim on you, too."

"But I did it first," she teased. They'd been through this before, and she had no doubt, they'd go through it again. Many times. And she knew he didn't mind that in a completely unorthodox move, she'd laid her claim first. In fact, secretly, Gabriella was pretty sure Kade liked the fact that she'd broken tradition. Because everything about their relationship went against tradition. Which, to her, was just one more thing that made it so special.

"And I did it last," he said, the way he always did as he pulled her close for a kiss. It didn't matter who did it first, or last, because the only thing that mattered was that he had a claim on her, and she had one on him. They were mated, and that would never change.

"It's a beautiful day," Gabriella said when he pulled away. "And you know I love these little hikes, but how would you feel about going for a run? Luke has the guests down at Blackwood Ranch today, so it's safe." She squeezed his arm, hoping he'd agree to run with her, but she knew he wouldn't. He clearly had something he wanted to talk about, which was why he'd convinced her to come out for a walk when they both had bread to bake and a meal to prepare for dinner.

"Maybe later." He shifted so he held her hand while they continued to walk. "I've been thinking a lot lately."

She smiled to herself. Finally, he was going to tell her what was on his mind. "Yes?"

"I want to visit Kira."

"Kira?" Of all the things she'd thought he'd say, that wasn't one of them, although she had to admit, she wasn't surprised to hear that he wanted to see Kira. Ever since his confrontation with his grandfather, there had been questions. There was no doubt that the brothers believed their mother had experienced the love of a fated mate, but there did seem to be more than a little doubt surrounding Kira's situation. Kade didn't like to talk about it, but when Gabriella did bring it up, more and more, he wasn't shutting it down. She knew he was thinking about it. "I think it would be a great idea to go visit her," she said honestly. "Why now?"

"Do you know much about the bond between twins?"

She shook her head. "Not much, really. There weren't many twins in my clan."

"We have a stronger bond. A *much* stronger bond. We can sense things with each other, kind of like with a mate, but not quite. It's different."

She nodded. "And do you sense something with Kira?"

"That's the thing." He let go of her hand and walked a few steps away. "I'm not sure. After she left, I didn't shift for so long that I suppressed all of my instincts."

"I remember." Gabriella smiled wryly.

"But now..." He turned and reached for her hand again. "Now that I've embraced my bear again, things are starting to come back. At first, it was all about you and learning our connection." He squeezed her hands. "But now that I have a handle on that, there's something else. I keep getting this feeling."

"Kira?"

He nodded. "I think so. Yes."

"And is she in trouble?" She dreaded to ask the question. But at the same time, if there was even the slightest chance that Kade's sister was in trouble, they needed to go to her. Without question.

"That's the thing, babe. I don't know."

She stood on her tiptoes and kissed his nose. "Then we'll go. As soon as we can."

"Kade! Ella?"

A shout rang through the woods. A deer who'd been resting only a few feet away startled and ran into the trees.

"Chloe's got a set of lungs on her." Kade shook his head and laughed, but Gabriella could hear the panic in her friend's voice.

"We're here," she called.

A moment later, Chloe showed up, looking as if she'd run a marathon. "Where's your radio?" She pointed her own radio at Kade's chest in accusation. "You're supposed to have it on you at all times. Especially now with Harper—"

"Is she...?" Gabriella interrupted. "Is Harper okay?" She'd been released from the hospital a few weeks after Ella's attack, and for the last few months had been taking it easy.

Chloe nodded and then grabbed her into a big hug. "She is. It's time. Axel took her down to the hospital for their checkup, and she started having contractions. They're a month early still, but Axel called and said they were taking her into the delivery room."

"Now?"

"Now!" Chloe glanced at her watch. "Well, thirty minutes ago. Maybe if we hurry, we can be there in time to meet the baby."

"The baby!"

Gabriella linked arms with Chloe and started off toward the Den. She was only a few steps away when she realized that Kade wasn't with her. "Are you coming, Kade?"

He nodded but didn't move.

"Kade?" Chloe had stopped along with her and looked at both of them expectantly. "Come on," she said. "It's time."

"There's going to be a baby?" He looked dumbfounded, as if he'd just made the connection that yes, Axel and Harper were going to have a baby. There would be a little cub at the ridge and everything would change.

Gabriella held her breath. They hadn't talked about cubs yet.

"There is," she said slowly. "How do you feel about that? Cubs, I mean."

He exhaled a long breath and a smile crept across his handsome face. "I think it's going to be pretty awesome," he said after a moment.

Joy bloomed through her at his words. She crossed the distance between them and kissed his lips hard and fast. "I'm glad you said that," she said. "And you're really going to think it's awesome when it's *your* cub." She added the last part before she twirled on her foot and ran back to Chloe.

The women had already started skipping down the trail toward the Den and the promise of a new life when Kade finally realized what she'd said. "Wait!" he called after her. "Does that mean what I think it means?"

Joy filled her and without breaking her stride, Gabriella turned and blew her mate a kiss. It was the only answer he was going to get.

For now.

I hope you loved Kade's story! I think he more than found his match with Ella. Do you think she's teasing him about a cub? Or maybe she is pregnant? You can find out and meet the Jackson's little sister, Kira in Hers to Take.
You can read a sneak peek right after this...

For more love and happily ever afters, I have an exclusive sweet novella that's not for sale anywhere. You can read it HERE!

HERS TO TAKE

Please enjoy a sneak peek of Kira's story in Hers to Take!

"I really am sorry, ma'am. But as I've tried to explain, we just don't have any riverfront sites available for a unit your size." Kira Jackson spoke as sweetly as she could. Not that it mattered, because the woman who'd been demanding Kira upgrade her family's campsite to one of the premium spots still didn't look as though she was prepared to take no for an answer.

The truth was, even if Kira did have a campsite available in May—the start of the summer season—that would fit the nasty woman's monstrosity of an apartment on wheels, she likely still wouldn't have given it to her. Not that she was vindictive; it was just that reserving the prime spots for nice families who were on their once-in-a-lifetime family vacations to Yellowstone National Park was definitely more rewarding than giving them out to people like the woman in front of her, who'd been spewing all kinds of venom from the moment she'd walked up to Kira's window.

"I demand to speak to your manager." The woman slammed her fist on the counter.

With her practiced smile still on her face, Kira took a step back and turned away. *She could speak to a manager all right.* Too bad Kira *was* the manager. Not that she was about to volunteer that information. Because Kira seriously doubted it would make any difference to the woman.

"Sasha, there's a woman who would like to speak to you." Kira spoke through clenched teeth to her co-worker, who'd just returned from a break. Sasha instantly identified the problem. Sadly, it was a little too common for either of their liking.

"I'll handle this." Sasha patted Kira on the shoulder as she walked by. "Why don't you go check the wood supply?"

Kira knew enough to take the out when it was offered. With a sigh of relief, she left Sasha and the unreasonable woman behind and headed outside where they kept the overpriced boxes of wood they sold to the tourists who, despite the cramped campgrounds, wanted to feel as if they were really camping in Yellowstone.

Not that it was a bad place. Not at all. And besides the occasional bad guest, for the most part Kira enjoyed her job in Yellowstone. It was the perfect place for a bear shifter to hang out. Well, maybe not the *perfect* place. That would be back home in Jackson Valley with her family. But that was no longer an option.

She sighed and straightened her shoulders. There was no point dwelling on the fact that she likely wasn't welcome at home anymore. Especially considering it was her own fault. *No. Yellowstone was her home now.* And as far as places she could have picked to start over, it was pretty good.

Her job allowed her to work in the woods, where she could sneak off to let her bear run free when she needed to, which was less and less these days. She was relatively left alone to manage the Riverside campground on her own. As long as she was doing her job well, and running things efficiently, her bosses didn't seem to care what she did. The people she worked with were nice enough, which was a good thing because they lived together in a small grouping of even smaller cabins behind the registration office.

She inhaled deeply and let out the breath slowly before she walked toward the wood pile. Selling the boxes for twenty dollars each didn't deter the tourists from buying them up, and the office was getting low. With the holiday weekend around the corner, they would definitely need to stock up. Which meant Kira needed to split the logs and fill the boxes.

Sasha thought Kira was crazy for always volunteering for the job, but ever since she was a little girl, Kira had always loved splitting wood. Her two oldest brothers, Axel and Luke, always tried to tell her she was too little, and girls shouldn't try to do a boy's job. A theory their grandfather subscribed to as well. It was Kade, her twin brother, who'd let her try his ax for the first time and taught her how to hold it. They'd always had a special relationship. A twin bond.

They used to be inseparable.

Used to be.

Kira shook it off and forced herself to focus on the present. It was getting harder and harder to avoid thinking of her brothers, especially Kade, but she'd made her choice and she'd live with it. No matter what.

She picked up the ax, set up the first log and hefted the ax over her head before she swung her arms down. Hard.

The log split easily. She picked up the smaller piece and repeated the action again and again, until finally her arms began to strain from the effort. She could have kept going, but Sasha's voice stopped her.

"You're a machine."

Kira turned to see her friend leaning against the wall, watching with wide eyes. She made a show of wiping her brow, despite the fact that she'd barely worked up a sweat.

"You've barely been out here twenty minutes." Sasha walked toward her. "How did you do that so fast?"

Kira shrugged. "Once I get going, I just get into a groove or something. Besides, we needed wood, so..."

"Still." Sasha shook her head in disbelief. "You must have had some aggression to work out after Mrs. McCarthy."

"Was that her name?" Kira propped the ax up against the chopping block. "She was something else. How did you manage to make her happy?"

Sasha laughed. "I told her a riverfront spot had just opened up that you didn't know about."

Kira raised her eyebrows and listened with interest.

"I gave her site 58."

"Site 58? The one behind the old outhouses?"

Sasha nodded and Kira couldn't help but laugh. "But did you see the size of their trailer? It would only—"

"Just fit?" Sasha smiled an evil grin. "Exactly. They'd be able to back in, nice and tight to the toilets. I'd be surprised if they could see the lake at all once they get in there."

"You're evil."

"I think you mean evil genius."

"Of course that's what I meant." Kira laughed. "Thanks for taking care of that for me."

"That's what I'm here for. Besides, I was kind of hoping you'd be so thankful that you'd go out and meet the maintenance guy for me in the shower house."

Inwardly, Kira groaned. Dealing with Cranky Carl, as he was referred to by the campsite staff, was typically a job they drew straws for and it was Sasha's turn. The old guy was fairly handy, but he far preferred to complain about it first. For at least an hour.

"You owe me," Sasha reminded her.

"Okay." She pulled the elastic out of her thick black hair and refastened it into a ponytail. She hoped she didn't have too many wood chips stuck in her hair. "But you're boxing the wood."

"Deal." Sasha tossed her the keys to the quad they used to get around the campground and disappeared back inside. Likely before Kira could change her mind.

She'd done a lot worse, and Cranky Carl wasn't nearly as bad as her grandfather used to get when he got mad at her brothers when they were cubs. The three of them always could fire up the old man, almost as if they made a sport of it. Come to think of it, they probably did. Not that they would have told Kira. She had definitely been her grandfather's little princess. She could do no wrong.

Except once.

Dammit. Why were thoughts of home intruding on her life today? It had been almost two years since she'd left. Two years since her brothers had come looking for her. And two years since she'd turned her back and sent them away. And all for a mate.

No!

For a man she *thought* had been her fated mate. She'd been wrong. And now there was no going back. She'd made her choice, and she'd just have to live with it. Just as she'd turned her back on her twin brother, he'd very clearly done the same to her. For months, she'd tried to reach out to him. The connection they shared was heightened because of their twin bond. When they were in bear form, they should be able to sense each other. Especially if the other was in some sort of pain or distress. And she had been. Every day since she'd left home, Kira felt the pain of the loss deep in her gut.

But Kade had never reached out to her. Every chance she got, Kira would shift into her bear and run through the forest, calling out for her brother. Even with the distance between them, there should have been something. Some connection to let her know she wasn't alone.

But there'd been nothing. And she hadn't tried in months. *What was the point?*

She'd accepted her new life. Mostly. But days like today when the memories flooded back were hard.

Kira fired up the ATV and put it in gear, headed to the shower house where two of the stalls had been backing up. Dealing with Cranky Carl would be a good distraction; at least she wouldn't have to think about anything else but clogged drains and broken showers.

———

There were about a thousand other things Nash North would have rather been doing than sticking his hand down the clogged-up, nasty ass drain of a shower stall in a public campground. When he took the job as the resident handyman for the summer, he hadn't given the job description much thought. Or any thought, really. All Nash cared about was a place to stay and a few dollars in his pocket while he figured out his next move.

Now that he was elbow deep in other people's hair and some sort of sludge he probably didn't even want to identify, Nash was definitely second-guessing taking the job without paying any attention to what he'd be doing.

He wiggled his fingers around the clog and tried not to think about what he might actually be touching when his sharp senses tuned into the footsteps of someone approaching.

A female.

He didn't look up, but Nash wasn't surprised when a moment later a sexy, smooth voice, with just a hint of an edge, asked, "What exactly are you doing?"

Without removing his hand from the drain, he looked up into the dark eyes of a woman every bit as sexy as her voice. More so. She was tall, although not likely as tall as he was, with strong, luscious curves beneath her parks uniform. The animal inside him responded immediately to the sight of her long, thick ponytail hanging down her back, her arms crossed over her ample chest, and the fire in her eyes as she stared down at him.

Maybe the job wouldn't be so bad after all.

"I'm fixing your drain, darlin'."

She narrowed her eyes. "I'm not your darlin'. And you're not Cranky Carl."

"No." Nash latched on to a wad of hair and sludge in the drain and yanked. "I'm definitely not Carl." He grinned. "And I'm not cranky. But I just fixed your drain." He wiped his hand on a rag and stood.

Damn. The woman was even more impressive when she was directly in front of him. And she was definitely not human. He held out his now clean hand. "Nash North."

Her dark eyes narrowed and she took a moment to look him over. She could have taken all day as far as Nash was concerned. Her gaze felt good. Damn good. Because if she liked what she saw even half as much as he liked the sight of her, it was going to be an interesting summer indeed. Finally, she took his hand.

"Kira Jackson." Her grip was strong, her skin soft, her touch electric. "Where's Carl?"

"Cranky Carl?" He raised an eyebrow.

"I shouldn't have said that." Kira slipped her hand from his and Nash had to fight the instinct to grab it back. "It's just that Carl can be a little..."

"Cranky?"

She tipped her head and for a moment she looked as though she might disagree, but finally she nodded. "Yes. He can be a little cranky from time to time."

"Well then, I guess it's an appropriate nickname," Nash said. "I can't tell you where he is, but I was told that I was hired on because the man before me retired. So perhaps he's a little less cranky now?"

"One can only hope." Kira smiled reluctantly.

"At least for his wife's sake."

"Oh, I can't imagine Carl is married."

"Are you?" The question was out of his mouth so fast, and so smoothly, it clearly took her a second to process it. Nash could see when she did.

Kira shook her head, looked away and took a step to the side. "I don't think so."

"You don't think you're married?"

"Oh, I *know* I'm not married." Kira spun around, her eyes blazing, making them look even darker than before. "Not that it's any of your business."

He knew he was being forward and presumptuous, but that had never stopped him before. "Mated then?" Nash could have sworn he heard a growl come from deep within her. And in that moment, he knew. *A bear. Damn.* He should have seen it right away, but there was something about her. Her animal was muted somehow.

"How the...what...you..."

"Wolf."

"Wolf?" She almost spat out the word. Nash took a step back and crossed his arms over his chest.

"You don't have to sound so damned disgusted about it."

"No." Kira shook her head apologetically and closed her eyes for a moment. "That's not what I...sorry...I didn't realize."

And that's what was wrong. She *hadn't* realized he was a shifter. It was unusual for a shifter not to recognize another. Even a different species. But then again, he hadn't recognized her as a bear. Not right away, anyway.

"Is that going to be a problem?" Nash tilted his head and watched her for a moment while she clearly had an internal battle he didn't understand. "Because, judging by the look on your face...it might be a problem."

"No." Kira shook her head quickly and bit her bottom lip, an action that sent a flash of desire right to his core. *Damn. The woman was sexy and had no idea.* "It's fine. I was just taken off guard is all."

"Were you?" He took a step toward her. As he expected, she didn't back away. Bears never did. Kira straightened and her deep, dark eyes stared directly into his.

"I was preoccupied was all. I wasn't expecting to walk in here and find a *wolf*." It wasn't his imagination; there was definitely disdain laced through her voice. "I was coming to deal with a clogged shower and Cranky Carl. I was not expecting *you*."

Nash took another half step toward her and rubbed the stubble on his chin as he challenged her with, "Well, you got me, babe."

"I'm not your babe."

"Not yet."

"No." She shook her head and stepped toward him, straightening up to her full height. *Bear or not, he wanted her. Badly.* "This isn't happening." Nash expected her to step closer, closing the gap. In his experience, bears didn't back down. Especially to wolves. Instead, she turned and walked to the door before she looked back at him. "If you plan on keeping your job, this isn't going to happen." Kira gestured between them. "I don't know if you were told, but I'm the manager of this campground and won't tolerate—"

"Me?"

"No." She glared at him. "I won't tolerate your...your...this."

She bit her lip again and Nash tried not to react. She'd calm down, but she was right. If he wanted to keep his job—and he did—he couldn't afford to piss her off. Even if it was fun to watch her get riled up. And it was. If there was one thing Nash enjoyed, it was to have fun with a sexy woman. "I'm sorry." But he also knew when to swallow it and play the game and in this instance, he was all about the game. Especially if it meant keeping his job. "I came here to clean up a clogged shower." He gave her his most genuine smile. "I definitely wasn't expecting to meet a beautiful bear while I had my hand down the drain."

His words didn't make everything better, but Kira's shoulders lost some of the tension and she no longer looked as if she was going to go for his jugular.

"At any rate," he said, pouring on the charm, "I didn't mean to come on so strong. Please accept my apologies."

He waited for a moment while she considered it. Nash half expected her to say no and fire him, or at the very least storm out. Bears weren't known for their ability to calm down quickly or, especially when it came to wolves, be reasonable. But Kira was definitely not a usual bear. In fact, she was very different from any other bear he'd ever encountered. And he was intrigued. To say the least.

"Okay," she said after what seemed like a very long time. "I accept your apology." She nodded toward the drain he'd just unclogged. "Thanks for that."

Nash waited until she'd turned her head and taken a few steps toward the door before he let himself smile. *He was really going to like this job.*

"Oh, and before you go." Kira turned around so suddenly, Nash swallowed his smile. "Check the other drains, and I heard there was a toilet that needed snaking. Could you see to that?"

He resisted the urge to salute. "Absolutely."

She gave him a look and for a second, he thought she might say something else. Instead, Kira nodded. "Good."

Nash didn't even try to contain his smile as he watched her juicy curves in her tight khaki pants walking away. *Oh, yes. The summer was definitely turning around for the better.* Was it really only a few weeks ago he'd left his big brother and his pack in search of something....well, just *something?* Things certainly turned around. Clogged drains and toilets aside, not only did Nash have a job for the summer, he had a place to sleep, and with any luck, before long he'd have a very sexy she-bear to cuddle up with to keep that bed warm.

Chapter Two

"A wolf?"

Kira stalked toward the cabins where the staff lived. She'd driven the ATV back from the shower house faster than she should have. Faster than the vehicle should move, period. But she needed to burn off some steam. What she needed to do was shift and let her bear out. But she wasn't doing that.

Not anymore.

There was no point in shifting.

There hadn't been for a very long time. But she hadn't ever before felt the burn in her veins, the heat that coursed through her, threatening to consume her. Something about Nash had triggered a response in her that heightened the need to shift into her bear, to run, to feel the animal inside her.

It wasn't an option.

"Dammit." She kicked a stone in her path. "A bloody wolf."

"A wolf?"

Kira spun on her heel to see Sasha next to the wood pile. "Did you say there was a wolf? Here? In the campsite?"

"No." She had to think fast. After all, there was a wolf in the campsite, but not one Kira could talk about. "No," she told Sasha. "I was just thinking about something else."

"You're sure? You look concerned about something."

"I'm fine." Kira forced a smile she didn't feel. "And really, it's nothing. I was just thinking about something I read in the newsletter about the wolves in the park." That wasn't entirely a lie. She had been reading about the Yellowstone-wide wolf reintroduction project and how some packs had thrived while others had failed. Kira couldn't help but wonder which one of those packs Nash had come from. Or whether he was a Yellowstone wolf at all.

Not that she was going to ask.

She was *definitely not* going to ask him.

"Hello. Earth to Kira." Sasha waved a hand in front of her face. "Are you okay? You look like you've seen a ghost."

Not a ghost. A wolf. A tall, sexy...

"I'm fine," Kira said. "I was just thinking about—"

"The shower room?" Sasha laughed. "What exactly went on over there?" Before Kira could come up with a decent excuse, Sasha's pretty face changed and her mouth fell into an O. "You met the new handyman, right?"

"What?"

"The new handyman. You met him, didn't you?"

"You knew Cranky Carl was gone?"

"Well, I didn't know *know*. But I'd heard." She winked. "And I saw a super hottie in a truck earlier, was that him? Judging by the look on your face, it was. It totally should have been me who went to check on the shower house. Damn."

Irritation rose in Kira. She didn't want there to be any look at all about her when it came to Nash. "What look on my face?"

Sasha did a little wiggly dance and her black curls bounced around her head. "*That* look!"

Kira stuck her hands on her hips and stared at her friend until she stopped dancing.

"Oh come on." Sasha laughed. "Judging by your face, I'd say you've just seen the sexiest man to ever set foot into this camp-site. Am I wrong?"

She wasn't wrong. "I guess Nash is—"

"Nash?" Sasha put her hand to her chest and swooned. "That's his name? Oh my God. Of course that's his name. He would have to have a totally hot name. It suits him, don't you think?"

Kira shook her head. She was not going to have this conver-sation. She didn't even want to think about him and his steel-gray eyes that seemed to see right through her and sense her need. Or the way his lean muscles filled out his parks uniform, or— "I guess he's attractive, if you like that type."

Sasha snorted a laugh. "That type? Of course I like that type. Who *doesn't* like that type? Damn, girl. I only saw him from a distance, but that is definitely a type I'd like to see close up. Really close up, if you know what I mean?"

Kira knew exactly what her friend meant, and it wasn't going to happen. If Sasha knew Nash was really a wolf shifter, she would freak out. *Probably.* The alternative was that her friend would be even more attracted to Nash and the last thing Kira needed to deal with that summer was a relationship between a wolf and a human. Particularly when that human was her friend and wolves were... well, wolves.

"He's kind of a jerk," Kira lied. Truthfully, she'd kind of liked Nash. Even if he was presumptuous and forward with her. Hell, that was probably why she liked him. Kira had always liked her men strong. Really strong. There was nothing sexier than a man who knew what he wanted and was willing to go after it. And wasn't that the problem? Nash *was* sexy. Too sexy.

"Really?" Sasha walked with Kira toward the cabin. "That's too bad, but then again, we're used to dealing with Cranky Carl. He can't be worse than that, right?"

Kira shrugged. "I guess we'll see. Turns out Carl retired. Not that anyone bothered to tell me. But then again, why would they? I'm only supposed to be in charge around here. Speaking of which..." She turned to Sasha. "Shouldn't you be in the office?"

"Conner's in there. I needed a few minutes away. He's so foul these days. Maybe we can start calling him Cranky Conner?"

Kira resisted the urge to laugh. It would be a fitting name for the man whose attitude had only deteriorated since Kira was promoted to campground manager over him. But now that she was manager, more than ever, she needed to maintain some sort of professionalism and try to make peace with Conner.

"I'll have to have a talk with him," she said. "Especially if it's becoming a problem to work with him."

If Kira was looking for her friend to tell her it would be okay, she was definitely looking in the wrong place. Sasha shook her head, put her hands on her hips and looked Kira straight in the eye. "It's not going to be a problem. I'm sorry. I'm not trying to be a whiney employee or make trouble when there isn't any, but he's so hard to work with, Kira. I'll do my best with him but he's going to need to sort himself out, or I'm going to tell him how to—"

"No." Kira held her hand up. "I don't think there's any need to tell Conner anything." At least not what Sasha wanted to tell him, which no doubt would only put him in a worse mood, or put Kira in the middle of a very unfortunate argument. "I'll handle it, okay?"

Sasha nodded, satisfied for the moment, and Kira put dealing with Conner on her to-do list. *Right under dealing with the Nash situation.* Not that it was a situation, but it would be if she didn't deal with it. There was no way she was going to have a *wolf* working with her. Not in her campground. *Especially not one as sexy as—no.* It had nothing to do with his sex appeal. At least that's what she'd have to keep telling herself.

Kira sighed and refocused on her friend. "Take your break early then. I'll take over in the office and if I get the chance, I'll talk to Conner, okay?"

Sasha skipped off in the direction of the staff housing, and Kira resisted the urge to go with her. The promotion from last summer had been unexpected, and not necessarily what she would have chosen for herself, but it was a good job and considering she didn't have a whole lot of other choices—like going home—she needed to make the best of it. If that meant making some hard decisions and having some even harder conversations, that's just what she would do. But it didn't mean she had to like it.

Kira was just about to go inside the camp office when a green truck pulling into the staff parking lot stopped her. *Nash.*

She waited and watched while he hopped out of the cab, grabbed a duffel bag from the box of his truck and headed toward the south cabin.

Her cabin.

Oh hell no.

Of course, if Nash was the new resident handyman, he'd need a place to stay and although the thought had crossed her mind, she certainly hadn't considered the fact that he'd take the spare room in the south cabin, where she stayed. Employee lodging was co-ed, and generally the rooms were assigned based on availability. *Surely there must be another vacant room in one of the other cabins?*

Kira's entire body stiffened, and she did her best to ignore the surge of desire that had shot through her at the idea of only a thin wall separating Nash's bed from hers. *No.* She could not allow herself to feel anything for him. He was a wolf, for goodness' sake.

An incredibly hot wolf, the little voice in her head chimed in.

As if he sensed her, Nash chose that moment to turn and see Kira watching him.

Even from a distance, she could see the flash of his teeth as he grinned at her, the heat in his eyes. *No.* She turned away and slammed the office door against the wall as she opened it and went inside. She had a phone call to make. Because there was *no* way she could have Nash in such close proximity.

Nash knew he should probably back off when it came to Kira. Especially considering she'd turned out to be his boss. Sort of. Either way, she was the manager of the campground, and even if he didn't report directly to her, it probably wouldn't be a good idea to piss her off.

But even though he knew logically he shouldn't push her so hard, he couldn't stop himself. From the moment he'd laid eyes on those curves and thick, juicy lips, he knew he wouldn't rest until he'd had a taste of her. At the very least.

The moment he'd opened the door and hopped out of the truck, he'd sensed her. There was no mistaking her scent. She was delicious. Her animal was faint, but it was there. As if she'd been denying or neglecting it. He knew she stood there watching him, because even if she tried to pretend it didn't exist, there was no mistaking the scent of desire. Kira was definitely not going to come to it easily, and that would be half the fun, but she wanted him just as bad as he wanted her. They both felt it. Of that, Nash had no doubt.

Finally, he turned and grinned at her. Just as he expected, she turned and walked inside. He let her go. For now.

She would be a challenge, that was for sure. But if there was one thing Nash liked, it was a challenge. Especially one in the form of a feisty she-bear. He'd never been with a bear. Hell, he'd never even considered it. In his pack, the focus was on breeding and expanding the population.

When wolves had been reintroduced to Yellowstone in 1995, it had been controversial among the shifter community. Not everyone thought it was a good idea. Packs were divided and families split. Nash's family was pro-reintroduction and as a pack, they'd made it a priority to make the program successful. Which, for Nash and his brother meant mating and breeding with other wolves to further the population. No exceptions. If it wasn't a priority to find a suitable mate, there was no room in the pack for you.

It's not that Nash was against mating with another wolf. Not at all. He just didn't think it should be forced upon him. His brother, the alpha, disagreed. When Nash refused to accept the female Nolan had chosen for him, he'd been cast out. Not that those were the exact words Nolan used.

"Take some time, Nash," he said. "Get it out of your system, whatever it is. And when you're ready, come home, take a mate and do the right thing."

The right thing. Whatever that was.

And that was the problem. Nash and Nolan had very different opinions on what exactly that was.

Nash walked into the cabin he'd been assigned and pushed thoughts of Nolan to the back of his mind. He was going to take the summer off, just the way his brother had suggested, and maybe when the seasons changed again, he might feel differently about his future. It was doubtful, but for his family, his pack, he'd give it a shot. Nash wasn't ready to completely close the door on his family. He knew what his decisions would mean for his future as well as his pack. And he still wasn't sure he was ready to turn his back on everything he'd ever known.

"Hey. You must be Nash."

A woman appeared in what looked to be the direction of the kitchen and smiled at him. She was petite, with deep-brown eyes and creamy dark skin that reminded Nash of a rich cup of hot chocolate.

"I am." He smiled at the beauty and offered his hand. "And you are?"

"Sasha. I work in the office. Welcome to Riverside."

"Thank you, Sasha." He dropped his bag at his feet and leaned against the wall next to her. She smelled floral and feminine. And human. Very different from Kira's earthy fresh scent. "It's good to be here. I'm looking forward to settling in. Do you happen to know which room is mine?"

"I'd be happy to show you."

She was cute, that was for sure, but Nash didn't feel the tug of arousal when he looked at her. "Oh, I'm sure you have work to do," he said smoothly. "I can find it." *There was only one female he wanted showing him any kind of bedroom.*

Sasha didn't bother hiding her disappointment. "It's the last room on the right." She pointed to a small hallway. "There's only two rooms over there, so you'll see it."

"And who has the other room?" He picked up his duffel. "Anything I should know about my neighbor?"

"That's Kira's room."

"Kira?" *Things were getting more and more interesting.*

"Yup. I think there's an extra room in the other cabin, if you'd rather—"

"No." Nash let a smile take over his face. "This is perfect." He started to walk in the direction she'd pointed. "I'll get settled and I'm sure I'll see you later, Sasha." He shot her one last smile and went to unpack.

A bear and a wolf…two strong alphas…how will that play out? I'm willing to bet a few sparks are going to fly! Find out for yourself and read the rest Hers to Take!

ABOUT THE AUTHOR

Elena Aitken is a USA Today Bestselling Author of more than forty romance and women's fiction novels. The mother of 'grown up' twins, Elena now lives with her very own mountain man in the heart of the very mountains she writes about. She can often be found with her toes in the lake and a glass of wine in her hand, dreaming up her next book and working on her own happily ever after.

To learn more about Elena:
www.elenaaitken.com
elena@elenaaitken.com